SLaSH anD GraB

Tyler Craig

Prince Harles Publishing

contents

Dedicated to the memories of Ruby Sue, Becca, Stella and Deja

Prologue

December 20th, 1950. 5:17 PM

Four girls sat in a circle drinking wine on the living room floor. They were gossiping about life and school and who the cutest boys were in their ethics class. Typical conversation for a group of twenty-year-old female college students when homework wasn't on their mind. It was Christmas break, after all. No classes would be attended in the morning.

That was reason enough for celebration, as jazz music echoed through the upstairs apartment from a record player behind them. Laughter and a wine fueled haze lulled them into a false sense of security. Seemingly without a care in the world between the four of them.

Unbeknownst to them, danger had been lurking outside for much of the day.

A package had been delivered to the girls in the early part of the afternoon with a note attached that read; "Hope this makes up for missing your flight. ?" Inside were four bottles of wine that the girls opened immediately. All four of them had their flights home canceled that afternoon, so they decided to spend the day together. This was the perfect gift to get their minds off of their families that they so dearly missed.

As they got lost in the sounds of the music and the bottom of their wineglasses, not a single one of them could sense what was about to happen as a man braved the winter weather outside. A blanket of snow—from the freak storm that pounded the city a day earli-er—masked the sound of any excess noise from the world beyond their party. If not for the weather, this party wouldn't even be happening. Each of the four girls would be back in the comfort and safety of their families' homes by now.

He waited until he heard the corkscrew pop open the first bottle before he scaled a ladder underneath an open bedroom window of the two-story townhouse. Not for the fun and warmth inside, but for something else entirely.

Through the window, he could see his prize. The very thing he was going through all of this trouble for. An item that would immediately change his life for the better.

He stumbled upon entry after climbing in through the window, hitting the floor with a thump. Spooked, he paused with bated breath. Once he heard the clinking of glasses from a post semester cheers in the other room, he exhaled a sigh of relief and kept on. His plan was definitely in motion.

A faint smile crossed his face at the sight of the bright green ques-tion mark painted on the wall above the bed. It brought back fond memories of times past. Which made him once again think about retreating. But he had come this far. He would not turn around now empty-handed.

Determined, he picked himself back up and found what he was after. It was behind glass. Nonetheless, he had come prepared. With the butt end of his Scout's hatchet, he smashed through the barrier. Retrieving what he had come for.

A familiar laugh made its way down the hallway. One that brought both joy and pain to the forefront of his mind. Suddenly, an icy cold feeling shot through his veins that had nothing to do with the temperature outside. That laugh was too much for him to keep his composure as his bottom lip started to quiver with emotion. How was it she had moved on while she still kept his painting on her wall?

The enticing sounds of the voices and music that emitted from down the hall had lured him to do more than he should have. Eyeballing the painted question mark one more time made up his mind for him. He already had what he had come for, yet that didn't stop him. He wanted revenge now. For not only his broken heart but also for the shame in which he felt after it was broken. His dignity was gone. He was not supposed to lose. Revenge was definitely in order.

Through an anger and hate filled trance, the thrusts came quickly. Violently. Not fully realizing what he had done until he saw the blood that was now smothering his hands. He dropped the knife he somehow managed to grab from somewhere, looking around in horror at the scene that now filled his eyes.

He wrenched the scarf off of one of the girls' necks to wipe his hands clean. A check of his pocket let him know his prize was still in his possession. One last look at his former flame lying dead on the floor left a lump in his throat. Guilt now clouded his vision as he hastily made his way back to the bedroom.

Towards the window.

Towards freedom.

COLUMBIA HEIGHTS, WASHINGTON D.C.

December 20th, 1950. 11:53 PM

I f it bleeds, it ledes. That's what the fourth estate says, at least. Well, we definitely had ourselves a bleeder here. Make that four, to be exact. A blood bath the likes we haven't seen in this city for a long, long time. Or so we were told.

"Denver and Diamond, coming up," I said with my badge showing in front of me as we ascended the stairs into the second-floor suite.

My partner's face instantly turned a pale white as we rounded the corner and the bodies of four colored girls sprawled on the floor came into view.

This was no recreational killer, that much was true. This guy meant business. His aggression spared nothing on these girls.

The only thing that came to my mind was that I hoped they didn't suffer. But with the amount of blood that was sprayed all throughout the room, I highly doubted that. Though I didn't have the guts to tell him, the sight was almost too much for me to handle too as I professionally turned my head and stifled a bile induced cough.

With a killing as brutal as this, tensions were higher than they would be at a normal crime scene. Hence the warning I shouted as we came up the stairs. It's always a good idea to announce yourself when entering an active crime scene. You never know what you might face when you round the corner. Criminals aren't the brightest, and who knows if this guy had gotten his fill yet.

Speaking of the fourth estate, they were already sniffing around the structure like the bloodhounds that they thought they were. We had to fight off questions and photographers just to get through to the front door. They were already taking the facts and putting their own spin on it the way they always seem to do without even knowing any of the details yet.

They were taking whatever conversations they could overhear outside of the house and running with it. I could hear them spewing their theories to each other from the front lawn as we walked up the path—calling it the worst injustice since that poor man was beaten to death by those Marines outside the White House back in 1919.

I don't think I'd take it that far, though. That was in the middle of a city-wide race riot, after all. And so far, this didn't seem to be racially biased. There were no messages of hate scrawled onto the walls, or anything else of that nature to make me believe that it was. But what did I know? I had only just arrived on the scene with my partner. It's probably a bit too early to tell if it is or it isn't. I just hated agreeing with the press, to be honest with you. I can only imagine what tomorrow's headlines are going to read.

Racial tensions are always high in this town, it seems, especially on the site of a university that is primarily full of colored students. But this didn't have that feel to me. I couldn't tell you why my gut was telling me what it was, but I didn't see any ulterior motives other than cold-blooded murder when I first stepped foot onto the scene. The amount of blood that was seemingly everywhere screamed brutality, but there's always a backstory that leads up to the point of no return. That's what we were here to piece together.

I often go with my gut instincts when first arriving at a fresh crime scene. And usually when my gut tells me something, I tend to listen.

I'm Max Denver. My partner here is Cole Diamond. We work Homicide for the Metropolitan Police Department in Washington D.C. We've only just begun working together recently, actually. He's new to the suit, and I'm the lucky one that got picked to show him the ropes.

It's hard moving from one partner to another, especially when you were with your last partner for over twenty years, but we'll get it figured out. Not like I have any other choice. 'Ol Jackie Boy is retired now, and he isn't going to be walking through the door anytime soon to join me, either. So, I'm stuck with the kid whether I like it or not.

This is only our third official case together, and his first with multiple victims. So, I really have to keep an eye on him. Weak stomach and all. Comes with the territory. I was pretty shaken on my first case, but that's a whole different story.

Diamond got to assist on a case me and my old partner closed a few months back. One that involved a certain high-ranking city official. You may recall reading about it in the papers. But that's old news. Today we're here because some sicko decided he wanted to carve up four coeds on the campus of Howard University.

Murders take place in this town nearly every day. But it's different when four students in the prime of their lives are cut down before their time. That makes people stand up and take notice. And after these vultures—with their cameras and their flashbulbs—get their shots in the morning papers, a whole hell of a lot of people are going to notice. And that's going to put the pressure on me and Cole.

Let's just hope none of them sneak behind the tape and get any photos from the actual scene. Those would be the bloodiest photos to hit the rags since the footage from Omaha Beach.

And nobody wants to relive that.

COLUMBIA HEIGHTS

December 20th, 11:55 PM

The call came in at a little before midnight. Right before knocking off time.

Go figure.

There was a disturbance reported along the Greek Village row of houses up in Columbia Heights around ten. Somebody had called the university police to report a burglary. When the uniformed coppers arrived on the scene, they were greeted with four dead dollies inside, a bloody kitchen knife, and not much else. Paramedics would arrive next—and when they were unsuccessful—the call came into us.

It appeared that a young college girl had invited three of her best girlfriends over for a night of drinks for an end of the semester celebration. Only thing was, they never made it past their first round from the looks of things. There were four bottles of wine on the counter in the kitchen—making it appear that they had a whole night of drinking planned out—but only one of those bottles was empty. According to my math, that's enough for only four glasses of wine. One glass for each of them. For some reason, their little soiree was cut short.

No pun intended.

We were met with some hostility by a couple of campus cops guarding the front door who looked like they had barely graduated from diapers. Didn't surprise me though. I have never been one to concede a crime scene without a little blowback or attitude, either. Coppers are territorial when it comes to jurisdictions. But we got the call, so it was our case now. Regardless of what these two youngsters thought.

As soon as we breached the door, I turned to Cole and said, "Diamond, close your eyes and tell me what you see."

"Um," he said with hesitation, "I see four dead bodies, Sir?"

This is something that I've been working on with him. It was the way I learned from Jack back in my early days.

As a detective, you have to be able to read a room in a matter of seconds. Especially if you're there before the medical examiner. You have to be able to account for everything in the room upon first sight so you can jot it down in your notepad later. I told him that each crime scene was like a new puzzle for us to solve. Maybe there were better ways to teach a rook, but I didn't know any of them. This was the third crime scene we've worked together, and I still don't think I've gotten it through his head yet.

"Is that all you see?" I asked, shaking my head and wondering why I agreed to this whole drying out process in the first place. Quietly steaming—from both the lack of alcohol in my system and the lack of Diamond's common sense—I added, "and what did I tell you about calling me "Sir"?"

My frustration shouldn't be taken out on the kid—I know this—but sometimes it all seems like too much. New partner, no more drinking, and showing the ropes to a rookie all at once is a lot to take in. I'm bound to have a few slip ups from time to time. I am human, for Christ's sake.

He opened his eyes after my outburst and gave me the look of a puppy that had just been hollered at for having an accident on the floor. The kid aims to please, that's for sure.

As he scanned the room, he named off everything that was in plain view from the doorway; the four girls, the four bottles of wine and wine glasses, some papers that were strewn out on the kitchen counter next to—and under the wine bottles—and the kitchen knife, dead center on the wooden floor in between all four of the girls.

What I saw was four girls lying in the middle of the floor circled around the supposed murder weapon. Almost in a ritualistic fashion. From where I stood, I couldn't see any nicks or cuts on any of their arms. It didn't look like any of them had put up a fight at all, which had my mind spinning. First instinct is that they were drugged or subdued in some way. Only way the killer could get the drop on them how he did. Those were my thoughts. Now I wanted to see if the kid saw the same thing I did.

"And what does all of that tell you?" I asked.

"That the killer didn't mess around," he replied. "He came in, did the deed, and split. Nothing looks to be upset around the house. No furniture upended or broken glass, and the frame on the front door looks to be intact. That tells me they invited the killer in. Like he knew the girls. Maybe slipped 'em all a Mickey Finn or something."

"Very good, son. We might make a detective out of you yet," I said in a reassuring tone. I've found that works best for the kid. Constant reassurance isn't part of my normal vernacular, but like the wine that sat unopened on the kitchen counter, I too seemed to be getting better with age. "Now, why don't you go have a look in the kitchen and see if there isn't something else in there that can back up your theory?"

As he went off for the kitchen, I pulled my pen out of my pocket and crouched down next to the closest victim to the door. I wanted to inspect the stab wounds before the ME and crime scene technician got there.

I also did a once over of the room. Diamond was fair in his assessment. Nothing seemed to be upended or out of place. But there was a lot of damage to these girls. The amount of blood was remarkable. Spatter covered most of the walls and even parts of the ceiling, too. This looked personal to me. I'll have to check with Frank Allcott down at the morgue after he gets a hold of the bodies, but I'd be willing to slap a fiver down on it that one of these girls took the brunt of the attack.

I worked with pace, knowing that I had little time before the ME showed up. This would be my one chance to see the bodies where they lay. As soon as they arrived, we would be shooed away so they could get their pictures taken and the bodies carried away to the morgue.

It wasn't often that we beat the ME to a scene. Normally, by the time we get called in, there's already a good fifteen to twenty people ahead of us who have already been through the crime scene, disrupting and contaminating god knows what in the process. This was a nice change of pace for us. Getting to see the bodies where they lie instead of relying on pictures and autopsy reports. Which meant I needed to get to work. Nothing worse than having a peek at a crime scene, only to be rushed out before you've finished your search.

I got down on both knees, pulling the first victim's shirt to the side, when I heard a voice call up the stairs.

"Crime scene tech coming up. Here to take some photos."

I recognized the voice as Sarah, the Chalk Fairy. Guess this means I won't get a closer look at the victims after all.

COLUMBIA HEIGHTS
December 21st, 12:07 AM

"Cole, pack it up. It's time to go," I said as I glared at Sarah, got back up on my feet and walked out the front door. I wasn't mad at the fact that it was her. I was more annoyed with her timing. She just had to walk in right when I was about to get to the good stuff.

We started seeing each other again recently, but in order to keep a lid on things, we both decided to go about business as usual. Meaning plenty of jabs and verbal low blows when our paths met at a crime scene. If we started acting cordial to one another, people would start to assume things.

"Flattie, what'd you do? Get mad somebody didn't invite you to their drinking party?"

"Real nice, Sarah. The consummate professional, as always, I see," I growled back with a hint of a flirtatious smile that I hoped nobody else saw. "People have jobs to do and beds to get back to. Why don't you stop with the jawing and get to work? I'd like to be home before the sun comes up."

I quickly descended the stairs and hurried off to a corner of the front yard that wasn't currently occupied by any other cops or folks from the press, so I could sneak a pull. I figured Diamond could find his own way out. Besides, it was time to give a few more yards' length on the leash I had around his neck. He would learn nothing if I held his hand throughout every damn procedure.

"Whatcha got there?" A voice said from behind me as soon as the liquid hit my tongue. I had to choke it down in an attempt to not spit it back up like one of the college kids on this very campus probably would have.

Turning my head, I saw it was one of the greenies from the Howard University department. "Medicine," I said with a smirk that he probably couldn't see. "I've got me this terrible cough. Can't seem to go five minutes without a drop of the stuff."

"Seems to be going around. My mother has had it pretty bad for a couple of weeks now," he said in what seemed like a very honest reply.

I chuckled to myself at his inability to read my sarcasm before realizing he wasn't going to leave me to it. Probably for the best, anyway. I am supposed to be giving the stuff up. I took a few steps farther into the darkness, hoping that he would get the hint, but with each step I took, he took two more.

"What gives, rook? Ain't nobody tell you to leave a dick alone when they's pacing?" I said as I looked back over my shoulder with another look that was probably lost in the darkness.

"Oh, I'm sorry, Sir," he said with the sincerity of a four-year-old. "I didn't mean to intrude. I just wanted to pick your brain for a few minutes. I've dreamt of becoming a detective for as long as I can remember. I just wanted to get your perspective on things up there."

"Well, seeing as I had about two minutes to look around before I was shooed out, I ain't got much to go on. How old are you anyway, kid?"

"I'm twenty-two, Sir. This is my first week on the job," he returned proudly, as if I was supposed to roll out a red carpet and bring the press over to this side of the yard to give him an interview.

"Oh, yeah? I couldn't tell," I said with a laugh. "But in all honesty, kid, I don't think I'm the best role model for you. You don't want to learn from me. I've got an attitude that would make a guard dog blush, and my patience is even worse. Now what say you run along and go play detective with someone else."

The kid turned and started heading back towards the house without another word, just as I saw Diamond on his way to the front yard. Great, I thought. Now I got two puppy dogs to deal with.

He approached me just as I snuck my flask back into my pocket. I think I got it in there before he saw it. And before you ask, yes, I had myself a fall off the wagon. Just a little slip up, you might say.

I stopped off at a liquor store the other night on my way home to buy me a packet of spearmint and the bottle just ended up in my hand. Old habits die hard, I guess. But I couldn't let it go to waste, so I dump a few sips into my flask from time to time for when work gets ugly. Like it seems to be tonight.

By this time of the early morning, most of the press that had lined the street earlier had dissolved, save for one or two that were still hanging around, bumping gums with each other. A flash bulb would periodically go off from time to time as the photographers were still trying to get the right shots for the morning edition. I don't know if this was front page news or not for the *Post*, but I'd put a buck on it that some of these pictures would turn up somewhere in it.

It was the very early morning hours now though. They'd have to hurry and get the pictures developed if they were going to make the first edition. As much as I hated catching a case right at knocking off time, I was glad I wasn't a photog. That had to be about the most thankless job there was. Taking photographs of every situation possible, hoping one out of the thirty you snapped that day might be worth a dime to some editor. And that was after you stayed up all night in the darkroom processing them all. Not a lot of bang for your buck there.

"Colio, whatcha find out in the kitchen?" I asked, as he was finally within earshot of me, hoping that he had more luck than I did in our short time up there.

"There wasn't much to see. The kitchen sink looked to be pretty clean. There were a couple of plates left over from the last meal that was eaten, but no other glasses or anything. There was a sixer of Hamm's in the fridge, though. They pulled two cans out of the packaging. And I only found one empty in the trash can."

"Interesting." I thought aloud. "Them girls don't look like the type to knock back a can of suds to me. Maybe this is the first clue we should run with. Once we find out who they were, we'll check in on their friends and see who was keen on the Hamm's. This was personal. Whoever did this knew those girls well."

I never fully understood beer drinkers as I pondered the thought of the beer can in the trash, but then again, I wasn't exactly a social drinker, either. I liked my Scotch whiskey. Straight and to the point. I never saw the appeal in nursing my drinks. If I wanted to get happy, a few pulls off the bottle would do me just fine. With beer, I'd have to drink a whole six-pack just to catch a buzz. And there's no fun in that when you're sitting around the house drinking by yourself.

"Whatcha wanna do then, Max? It's too late to go knocking on doors now, dontcha think?" the kid asked. I could see that his eyelids were getting heavy. He was right, of course, but I think the motive behind the question was more personal than practical.

"Yeah, you're probably right, kid. And it's gonna be hard to track anybody down since they're all on break right now, anyway."

It was the week before Christmas and most of the campus would be pretty quiet for the next three weeks. That makes our job hard enough as it is but throw in the fact that this guy had to get his fill just as the worst storm of the year rolls through town doubles that. We definitely have our work cut out for us.

"My best bet is we should probably try to talk to admissions or someone from the school first thing tomorrow," I said, pointing off toward the direction of the main campus. "Start building a list of friends we can speak with. For now, though, let's wait this out as long as we can. We need to get them bottles and glasses into bags so we can enter them into evidence. And I want that can out of the trash, too. Maybe we can lift some prints off of it. Might be the break in the case that we need. Anything of note on those papers on the counter?"

"It didn't look like it, but we should bag them too, right?"

"You bet your ass we should," I stated. "Everything in that room is evidence. Whether or not it appears to be."

One of the worst parts of this job was waiting for the crime scene technicians and the medical examiners to finish their job. The meticulousness of it was very time consuming. We were on overtime, so at least we were getting paid double to be standing out there in the cold. A minor bonus for catching such a late case.

"Let's do a perimeter search. Maybe the killer ditched his can before he left the property," I suggested to the kid. "You go around the left, I'll go 'round the right. Meet you at the back of the house."

"Sounds good, Sir. I mean, Max. What am I looking for?"

"For starters, that beer can. But also, check for footprints, too. And blood. There should be a trail of blood coming from the house. There's no way this guy didn't wind up with no blood on him in one form or another. Right now is the best time to gather any of that type of evidence. If we wait too long, it might be gone by the time the snow melts."

"Roger that. I'll see you on the other side."

COLUMBIA HEIGHTS
12:15 AM

With my flashlight in hand, I set off around the right side of the house to look for any clues that might be helpful to our investigation. I didn't see any lights on in the downstairs unit, so I figured that the people who lived there must've been away. Though it was in the wee hours of the morning now, I expected they would be awake from all of the commotion upstairs if anybody was home. Maybe they all had gone home for their Christmas break as well. Narrows our witness list down a little bit, at least.

This all seemed a little too convenient, if you ask me. The killer could walk into a house where he was known—kill the inhabitants—then walk away scot free, knowing there weren't any witnesses around within a block of the campus to see what he had done. Seemed like we had a real smart one on our hands here. Which is never what you want to believe when you first catch a case.

The side of the house that I was searching had a small pathway smoothed down from years of foot traffic. There was barely enough room for me to walk down it without either bumping my shoulders against the wall of the house or the trees that lined the property. If the killer made his way down this path, there would be ample opportunities for him to leave a blood trail inadvertently. And so far, I wasn't seeing it.

There was plenty of trash along the path though, which is what I guess would be expected, seeing that this was a house full of college kids. Still, not much stood out that warranted me taking my evidence bags out of my pocket yet. Until I came across what looked like a copy of the school's newspaper—creased and trodden—on the ground in front of me. The front page of a weather-beaten edition of *The Hilltop* was staring back up at me as I made my way down the final steps of the path.

I checked the date; December 19th, 1950. It was yesterday's edition. The photograph on the page looked to me like a group of classmates taking their final exams, eager to be done with the semester and return home to see their loved ones. Maybe this could offer some names for us to run down. I thought it was strange that the paper would still issue an edition when most of the students would be home on break, but maybe this is why I'm a copper and not an editor.

I picked it up and placed it as gently as I could into one of my plastic evidence bags. Once I was in some light, I would be able to get a read on the faces in the picture. Maybe one of our girls was in it. We're going to have to identify them quickly so we can make a next of kin notification. And since these four girls were still here when most of their classmates had gone home for the holidays, that made me believe they were definitely not local.

I made it to the back of the house before Cole did, so I did some looking around in the fenced-in backyard while I waited.

A lot of the same back here, too. Trash seemed to litter the lawn in every direction I looked. There was a round bricked off area, which I assumed was a fire pit. It also seemed to serve as a trash receptacle, as the damn thing was full of aluminum beer cans. They looked clean too, telling me that there hadn't been a fire in the pit in quite some time. Not that this struck me as odd for it being late December, but why would there be a party going on back here this time of year without a proper heat source?

College kids do funny things, though. Just like when you see a group of them in the stands at a football game without their shirts on when it's below freezing. I chuckled to myself as I thought that I'm glad I'm over that macho growing up phase of my life. *I got a job, and I got a girl. There ain't nobody left to impress at my age.*

I poked around the pile with the toe of my shoe while the eerie feeling that I was being watched arose. Though I didn't see anybody on my search of the perimeter of the house, the sensation was still pretty apparent. I chalked it up to my nerves, and the fact that it was pitch black out in the backyard. I never got over my fear of darkness—even in adulthood—after watching Dracula when I was a child. Those nightmares still come back to haunt me from time to time. Even to this day. Funny, I can go toe to toe with the most dangerous people in the District, but stick me outside in the dark and all of a sudden I have to worry about soiling myself.

I tried to suppress that feeling as I got back to the job in front of me. There were various types of cans in the fire pit, but it looked like Hamm's was the beer of choice for this house. *There goes our first lead*, I sarcastically grumbled to myself.

Diamond rounded the corner from his side of the house at about that same time. The rustling of his shoes on the frostbitten grass snapped me out of my thoughts.

"Find anything?" I asked as he approached me.

"Not really, no. Just some trash, is all. No beer cans. And it's too dark to see if there was any blood left anywhere. How 'bout you? Any luck?"

"Same. I bagged a couple of items off the ground but didn't see anything that stood out at me. But have a look at this," I said, motioning him to the fire pit. "Looks like these girls must have stock in Hamm's or something."

"Well, I guess that throws out chasing down the beer can from the fridge, then."

I nodded in agreement and was about to add my two cents when I heard the noise of an engine turning over, which just about made me jump out of my boots. Who on earth would be making a trip anywhere at this hour? I turned around in time to see the taillights of a rusted-out coupe speed off down the alley.

I raced to the fence—hoping to catch a glimpse of the license plate, or at least get a read on the make and model of the car—but it was too late. The car had already rounded the corner and was back out on the street by the time I got to the fence.

"What on earth was that?" Cole asked once he caught up to me at the edge of the backyard.

"I ain't got no idea, kid, but I don't like it. When we get back to the car, radio it in. I gots me a feeling about this that ain't sitting right in my stomach."

"What about the cans in the fire pit? I don't think we have enough evidence bags to grab all of them tonight."

Dejectedly, I agreed with a nod, though I doubt he saw it in the darkness. He had a good point. I only had three bags on me, and each one could only hold one can each. We were going to need a 35-gallon bag at the least. There wasn't much more we could do out here tonight. Plus, I wanted to get a call in about that car that sped off. There was definitely something fishy about the timing of that.

"We'll have a better shot at this tomorrow," I said to my partner. "I'll go check in with Sarah and the university cops to see if they need anything else from us, but I think we should be good to call it a night."

I did one more quick visual with my flashlight around the perimeter of the yard. From where I was standing, there looked to be two ruts in the grass from a hand-truck or something that led directly to the back gate. That car speeding off had spooked me so much that I had forgotten why we were back there in the first place. It was probably too dark to see anything now, but first thing tomorrow morning, bet your ass I'll have a look at those tracks. This wasn't a coincidence.

If the killer went through there, he'd leave behind a clue for sure.

EDGEWOOD, WASHINGTON D.C.

December 17th, 11:52 PM

T he older of the two flat mates departed from his closed bedroom door and made a path to the living room. He saw his roommate sound asleep on the couch. A line of drool marched down his face towards the pillow like a line of worker ants gathering for their hive.

The pair had worked a double the day before, something the kid wasn't quite used to yet. Which was why he was planning this job for the two of them in the first place. Seeing how exhausted the kid was had got his mind thinking: he needed to get them on the path to riches and an early retirement.

If it weren't for the fact that he didn't have a car, he'd do all of this by himself. But the walk would be too far from their apartment. Not to mention—if he was spotted—fleeing the scene would become a lot harder on foot. And it would be a lot more suspicious looking for him if he were caught running out of the house by prying neighborly eyes. No, he definitely needed his friend for this.

Still, guilt clouded his senses, knowing what was at stake. Yet the dreams of a better life seemed to win the battle going on in his head.

Besides, the money they would fetch from this job would put both of them on a better path. And that's exactly what he promised the kid's mother he would do when he agreed to let the boy stay with him.

Sure, he got the kid a job flipping burgers with him at the diner, but there are no real wages out there for colored folks. Especially not colored kids their age. Not unless they wanted to move out to the hills and work in the mines. But that was a death sentence. If the mine didn't collapse on your head, the black lung would get you after enough time underground.

This "job" that he was planning was the only thing that would put the two of them on the right track in life. Whether or not it was legitimate.

Not that the younger boy couldn't take care of himself, but he had always treated him as his kid brother. And flipping burgers wasn't a life anybody should be proud of, no matter the color of your skin. Plus, a promise is a promise.

The kid was what you might call slow. He had enough of it together so he could hold down a job—and get a driver's license—but he was a little on the naïve side of life. Which had worked in the older man's favor on more than one occasion. It definitely helped when he was too hungover to go to work. All he had to do was tell his young friend to cover for him and he'd have the day off to recover.

But what he was asking the kid to do for him now was something that even he was having a hard time with. This wasn't just an extra shift at the diner. This was something that could land the both of them behind bars for a very long time if they weren't careful.

All of this uneasiness would change once they had their trophy in their possession. Their lives would be changed for the better. This one-of-a-kind opportunity was too good to pass up.

That's what he kept telling himself, at least.

ARLINGTON, VA

December 21st 10:03 AM

The next day, I woke up around ten, having had more of a nap than a restful night of sleep. Late night cases always do a number on my sleep cycle, setting a grouchy tone for the rest of the day. Add that to the fact that we didn't get any hits on the car we saw speeding off last night meant that my mood was going to be one for the ages. Poor Cole was going to be in for a wild ride today.

I telephoned Diamond and let him know I was going to take the rail all the way to the campus of Howard University and that he should pick up a car from the station and meet me there. I live on the other side of the river—a few miles across the state line out in Virginia—so it takes me some time to get into work most days.

It's going to be hard enough to track anybody down with most of the campus closed up for the break and even harder yet, seeing as we are going to be there right about lunch hour. I didn't want to waste any valuable time by going to the precinct first to meet Cole. It would be faster to go directly to the school.

As I suspected, Diamond was sitting in one of the black department issued '47 Deluxe Tudors waiting for me outside of the train depot as I disembarked the late morning train. Though I didn't ask him to do it, he was there to pick me up so he could drive us the rest of the way to the campus like I was royalty or something. Shaking my head as I walked towards him, I politely said thank you and got in. I have to learn when and where I pick my battles. Sober or not, this one seems to be even too petty for me to justify. I chalked it up to my lack of sleep and let it go as I grabbed my seat in the car.

I have been mostly dry for the past two months, but I still haven't looked into getting myself a vehicle yet. Probably should give that a second thought soon. It would make things a lot easier for me if I ever needed to get somewhere in a hurry.

As like most of us, I'm a creature of habit, so when the wife left and took our car with her, I became passenger dependent. Not that she needed it. The car, that is. Her new husband seems to be swimming in cash and probably bought her a new one, anyway. But I'm pretty sure it was a spite thing on her behalf. And I don't blame her. I would've done the same thing, I bet. But that was about the time I started heavily with the drink, so I never bought myself a new one. And I've done just fine so far without one. No need to fix what ain't broken, and all that jazz.

With Diamond behind the wheel and me across from him on the bench seat, we drove straight to the crime scene. I wanted to get an early crack at the admissions office, but that was going to have to wait since we were still waiting for positive IDs from all four of the victims. Which hopefully we will have before the day is over. The longer it takes to ID the girls, the harder it will be to track down the person who did this.

I figure this could be another chance to go through the crime scene in the light of day as well. See what we missed before they rushed us out last night. Also, it can be a learning opportunity for Cole, too, before we get into another lesson in questioning witnesses later on in the day.

I told him to go back to the kitchen area and really comb through the evidence left behind in there. I was specifically interested in the papers that were strewn about on the counter. Often, the break in a case comes from something as meaningless as one sheet of paper. Could be where a print had been left. Or sometimes it even could be the cause of ire from the killer themselves. Past due payments were second only to cheating spouses in our line of work.

I was going to tackle the part of the house that we haven't seen yet: the bedroom.

As we ascended the staircase to the crime scene for the second day in a row, I realized there were no uniforms monitoring the scene outside of the house. Which struck me as more than odd. There should've been coppers here overnight. Not only inside the unit, but out on the front lawn as well. Not only to keep the crime scene from getting contaminated, but also to keep the press away so they couldn't sneak in and snap pictures we didn't want the public to see. I pressed on anyway. Not my call, not my worry. Campus cops aren't used to the sort of treatment needed in a case of this magnitude. Still, I was a bit miffed, if I'm being honest.

The front door to the unit was wide open, so I announced our arrival as we hit the top of the stairs. Not hearing anything back from my announcement, I walked inside. The room looked mostly the same as it did last night, save for the four girls being removed.

I made a beeline straight to the bedroom and left Diamond to do his thing in the kitchen. The rest of the place wasn't very big for how large the living room/dining room area was. That part of the apartment was all open. A large single room. The only difference at all was that the living room had wooden floors while the kitchen and dining room floors were tiled. The short hallway that led to the sleeping areas was carpeted. So, naturally, I got down on my hands and knees to see if I could see any footprints that looked to be larger than any of the girls.

No dice. There didn't even appear to be any foot impressions at all on it. Must've been vacuumed recently. Which makes sense if a get together was planned. I know the wife used to make a big stink of things when we were about to entertain. One of the perks of being a bachelor for all those years was not giving a damn about what my place looked like. Though that has changed a bit with the presence of Sarah in my life now.

I crept into the bedroom on the right side of the hall first. Upon my initial look, I noticed what I assumed I would in a college girl's bedroom—a large dresser with a small vanity atop it, a Dansette record player that stood in the room's corner with a stack of 45's on their own table next to it, a bed, some posters on the wall, and a nightstand with a picture frame on top of it. The thing that stood out most to me was a giant bright green question mark that looked like it was painted directly on the wall right above the bed. This image seemed to be extremely out of fashion with the rest of the room's décor. Making a mental note, I moved on.

I searched the dresser first. Opening each drawer to see if anything looked to be disturbed. This is one thing I will never get used to doing no matter how many cases I catch. Looking into someone's personal life and finances is one thing but combing through the underwear drawers of victims—especially ones as young as this—is something I will always feel dirty about doing. But because we still don't know what the motive is for the killings, it is a necessary sin that I have to do to make sure that I leave no stone unturned.

Nothing looked to be out of place, so I moved on to the next thing in the room. It wasn't until I got around to inspecting the picture frame on the nightstand next to the bed that I noticed I was on to something. Suddenly, the hairs on the back of my neck were standing at attention. I felt a slight breeze from the window next to the table that was left open about a quarter of an inch. This was where the killer got into the house. No person in their right mind would leave their window open—even just a crack—during the snowstorm that we just had.

I, of course, changed my perspective from the picture frame to the window. Since the front door looked to be undisturbed, this had to be where the killer entered. It really was the only place that made any sense and backed my suspicion that the killer didn't use the front door. Unless he truly was invited in, like Cole suggested last night. But I doubted that assessment after seeing the open window.

Not wanting to contaminate any prints that might have been left behind, I left it alone. As soon as we find whoever is supposed to be guarding the crime scene, I'll have them come in and dust for prints on the inside and outside of the window. I then turned my focus back to the picture frame on the nightstand.

The glass looked like it had been smashed, opening up the frame for whoever was trying to retrieve its contents. Shards of glass were strewn across the carpet and on top of the blankets of the bed. A note in cursive writing was all that was left in the frame now. Reading: *A Babe for my Babe. Love Daddy.*

I'll have to remember to check with Sarah to see if she got any photographs of this part of the house, but just in case, I bagged the frame and headed over to the bedroom across the hall.

It looked very much the same as the room I just came from, minus the record player. A stitched line from the Gospel of David hung from the wall above the bed. It was the lone item hanging on the otherwise bare walls. I did a quick inventory of the contents of the dresser, noting that everything looked to be undisturbed, and went back out to join Cole in the kitchen.

The kid already had all the items from the counter bagged into evidence bags. He grabbed the entire trash can instead of only the can of Hamm's that I had requested. Smart move, actually. As I approached, he was jotting something down in his notepad.

"Whatcha got? Find anything useful?"

"No, not really. Same as last night. I just wanted to leave a note for the officers to dust for prints in and around the kitchen. Specifically, the refrigerator and over here on the counter."

"While you're at it, leave a note to have them dust the window ledge in the bedroom, too. The window was left open a crack, and I'm thinking now that the killer could've come in through there."

"But it's a second story unit, Max. How'd you expect someone to climb in through an upstairs window?" The kid was asking the right questions, at least.

"The same way anybody else would climb through an upstairs window, you idiot. With a ladder." I said in a matter-of-fact tone. "Last night, I saw some drag marks out in the backyard that led to the gate at the back of the property. Those marks could've been caused by a ladder being drug out to be disposed. Or even to be thrown into the back of a truck, for all we know. The gate looked to lead to an alley, so we'll have to go check and see what we can find out there before we head over to the admissions office later this afternoon."

Cole looked at me with understanding in his eyes for once. "Should we go have a look now, then?"

"Probably. I'm still wondering where the uniforms are at. But we can't sit around here all day and wait. Why don't you head down to the car and radio into the station? Find out who's supposed to be here."

As he headed down the stairs, I took one more glance over the area. There was a clue here somewhere. Something that hasn't let itself be known yet, but I know it's here somewhere. The blood stains on the floor didn't reveal any footprints letting me know where the killer stood while he carved those poor girls up. But the center of the room where the knife was found was completely void of any blood. Bringing my mind full circle to where it was last night. But if this was ritualistic, there would be a lot more than just blood splattered around the living room. And that clearly wasn't the case.

Not everything you come across as strange reveals itself to you in the end. It was definitely odd, yes, but it doesn't get me any closer to finding out who did this in the least. All it tells me is there had to be a blood trail somewhere on the property.

Crouching down—as I was last night before Sarah showed up—I tried to get the same view that the girls had as the life escaped their bodies. *What did they see? What did they hear?* I asked myself as I got down on my knees.

Nothing stood out to me. All I saw were the walls and the ceiling in front, and above, where they were lying last night. Nothing looked out of place, telling me they didn't put up much of a struggle as they clung to life as the blood poured out of their bodies. This entire case had me baffled.

How did one man do all of this without these girls resisting at all? It just doesn't make one lick of sense to me.

Empathy wasn't lost on me, but at the moment, I failed to sense what they sensed as they were expiring. And it was frustrating me beyond belief. The only thing that stood out at all was the lone dry spot in the middle of the floor. That still had me perplexed. But I know it doesn't lead to the answers I'm after right now. We need to find the killer as soon as we can. Staring at the clean spot on the floor doesn't do that. I need to clear my head and think. Maybe another shot is in order. That always seems to clear my mind and lets me focus.

As I stood and headed back downstairs, I snuck a pull off my flask. I know that I'm missing something, but I can't put my finger on it. It is so blatantly obvious that it is right there in front of me and God—out in the open—but I just can't find it. Hopefully, Sarah snapped enough photographs to find what I was missing. Sometimes a different point of view can make all the difference in the world.

I just hoped that this was one of those times. If not, I think we might not solve this one.

EDGEWOOD

December 19th, 4:54 PM

"I'm telling you, Boyd, it's the real deal," Jimmy beamed. His eyes were wide as he recalled the baseball card his girlfriend, Ruby-Sue, had showed him the night before. "I saw it with my own two eyes."

"No way, you're lying. There were only like 150 of those even made."

"It's real, alright. A 1933 Goudey Babe Ruth. She even showed me the powder that was still stuck on the back of it from the stick of gum it was up against in the packaging."

"I don't believe you," Boyd insisted. "How did she get so lucky to end up with one of 'em, while it's us two who'd actually appreciate it? That's better odds than winning the sweepstakes!"

"It's real, alright," Jimmy insisted again, trying to get the point across to his friend. "Besides, why would she show it to me if it weren't? She already has me. It's not like she was using it to try to impress me."

Lost in the daydream of what a card like that would feel like in his hands, Boyd went quiet. Jimmy left him to his thoughts as he, himself, tried to come up with an easy way to get the young, naïve kid to go along with the plan he was about to ask him.

"Where'd she even get it from?" The anxious Boyd finally asked.

"She told me it was her father's. He gave it to her when he got sick a few years back. After he died last year, her mother told her to hang on to it. Told her that she could probably sell it if she ever fell on hard times after college."

"What luck!" Boyd exclaimed. He still wasn't sure he believed if what his friend was telling him was true or not.

"Well, what if her luck became ours?" Jimmy asked.

"I'm the world's most unlucky fella," Boyd said with a sad look and a shake of his head. "You already know this, Jimmy. Besides, we'd need 10 Gees to be able to afford one of them, and that ain't happening anytime soon."

Jimmy smiled at his friend. Not because he agreed with his statement, but because he knew that if they pulled this off, he would be the one taking home most of the riches. He'd made it a practice of taking advantage of his gullible friend. This time would be no different.

"I'm saying we make it our own luck and steal it. From Ruby-Sue."

"But that's your girl, Jimmy!" Boyd exclaimed once again. His eyes looking like they were about to bug out of his skull.

"We only been going steady a couple of weeks now. Not like I can't find another girl. You see how many girls there are in this city?"

"I dunno," Boyd said as he held his head between his hands and stared down directly between his two feet. "Seems kinda risky. Dontcha think?"

"Not at all," Jimmy said with the confidence of a tried and trusted cat burglar. "She'll be out of town, just like everyone else on that campus. You drive me there and let me out a block away. I'll break in and take it, then meet you back at the car. Easy as that."

Boyd stared at the floor in their living room and took a big gulp out of the can of beer he was holding in his hand. Weighing out all of his options. He had gone along with plenty of Jimmy's plans before, but this one could actually get the both of them into a lot of trouble. Jimmy had never steered him wrong before, though. Why would he do it now?

"And you think this plan will work?" Boyd finally asked after another round of silent thinking. He was skeptical of his friend's words, but once again, he had never wronged him in the past.

"Of course it will. Ruby Sue is leaving for Philly tomorrow morning," Jimmy explained. The smirk on his face conveyed he was rather confident that his plan was foolproof.

"She already told me that everybody else in the house has already left for the holidays," Jimmy continued. "The place will be deserted. And with the trees on either side of it—even if someone is in one of the houses on either side—nobody will be able to see a thing. It'll be like taking candy from a baby. That's how easy it will be. I'll be in and out in no more than five minutes."

Boyd went silent once again. His juvenile mind wasn't capable of this type of dilemma. "Okay, if you say so. I guess you're right. How hard could it be, right?" Boyd asked tentatively, taking another large drink from the can. He wasn't feeling as confident as his roommate was. But after the last time he let Jimmy down, he wasn't sure if he could ever do that to him again. "So, when are we gonna do this?"

"Tomorrow night. As soon as the sun goes down," Jimmy said with that same smirk on his face as before. He was already planning out what he would spend his portion of the money on.

Of course, he would take the larger cut since it was his plan, and he was doing all the heavy lifting. Boyd would be happy with a thousand dollars, he thought. It's more money than he would ever think he could earn.

"We'll take the day off from the diner to get ourselves ready. So get some sleep tonight, Boyd. Tomorrow, our lives change forever."

COLUMBIA HEIGTHS

December 21st, 12:17 PM

O fficer's Bryce Davis and Alvin Miller were finally walking up the stairs to the second-floor unit just as I was heading back down from the apartment. They claimed the reason they weren't guarding the door was because they were on their lunch break. I shook my head and let it slide. It was too early in the day to be butting heads with people, especially those two idiots. That was a losing battle I didn't particularly want at this hour of the day, though it took more willpower than I knew I had to keep my mouth shut and focus on the goal in front of me.

I shouldn't be so harsh. They're both great guys—nice to talk to if you've got some time to kill—but they might be two of the dumbest people I've ever met. And I'm not the only one who thinks this, either. I've heard a few of the fellas around the station refer to them as Moe and Curly, stating that the only thing they were missing was Larry. But comedy isn't quite the goal of the Metropolitan Police Department.

Especially not today when we are tasked with finding this ruthless killer.

Regardless of my feelings towards them, I swallowed my pride and told them about the notes we had left for them—hoping the two numbskulls would actually get the fingerprint dusting done around the house—and how we had already bagged all the evidence Cole and I had talked about last night.

Now that I know the window was looking more and more like the point of entry of the killer, we will have more to focus on in the backyard besides the empty beer cans that were left in the fire pit. Which I was extremely happy about. I've gone down that road before of trying to track down and identify fifteen to twenty different perps via their fingerprints. To say it's usually a waste of time is an understatement. Especially here when we're on the campus of a university. There's no telling how many people have come through this property all in the name of catching a buzz. This will save us countless man hours and department funds by not having to waste resources on what would most likely be a dead end.

I'm now focusing my attention on finding a ladder, which I'm assuming the killer used to climb through the window. Which might also explain the two grooves that I saw in the snow last night as well. There had to have been a way for the perp to enter through the second-story window. He couldn't have scaled the wall without some sort of device for climbing.

I made my way to the back of the house to have a look at the second-story window from the outside. As I expected, the two grooves in the lawn that I saw last night led directly to the base of the wall. There were two indents in the frozen ground right below the window, signifying where the ladder was placed.

There looked to be some blood droplets on the grass under the window. Once again, I was right. The killer was leaving us a blood trail. They seemed to follow the direct path of the footprints and drag marks. I followed the grooves that were apparent in the snow to the gate that led to the alley. Every few feet, I would catch sight of another drop of blood through the melting snow, but there wasn't much. Not nearly as much as I thought there should be. Especially with how much the blood seemed to fly throughout the room while he stabbed them. *How did he keep it all off of him?*

And it wasn't coming from the killer's shoes either. The spots would be much bigger if they were. These spots ranged in size from a dime to a quarter. If it were shoe prints, they would be at least the size of a dollar bill. Maybe it was dripping off of an article of clothing or something similar. I took a mental note and made my way through the gate to the alley, perplexed.

I looked to my left once I went through the gate into the alley. The ladder in question seemed to lean up against a fence. It was just lying there out in the open—not even covered up or anything—like the killer just left it be and booked it off the premises.

There appeared to be some dark spots on the light, tan-colored wood that caught my eye as I walked closer to it. The blood droplets on the ground—that I was still following—led directly to the spot I was headed to now. I studied each one as I passed over them, noting in my mind where each one was located so I could point out where Sarah would need to focus her camera on.

The blood trail seems to stop at the ladder, which made me want to take a closer look. This was definitely what he used to get in and out of the house with. There were dried blood markings all over the thing. This whole section of the alley was now a crime scene, making me wonder if the car we saw speeding off last night happened to be the getaway vehicle.

In the dust of the alley, I found several footprints surrounding the ladder. Two sets looked like they came directly from the backyard of the crime scene house: mine and the killers. But one set led away from the fence, right towards the spot where I saw the car last night. The damn snow that melted overnight must have washed away the tire tracks, leaving me with a pair of footprints that lead to nowhere. But I know what I saw. There was most definitely a car right here last night. Almost as if the driver was camped out in it, watching us during our investigation.

We already alerted an APB on the rusted-out coupe, which is something I can't hurry along no matter how much my temper starts to flair. Feeling disappointed, I returned to the ladder to get a closer look at the footprints there.

From my estimate, both sets looked to be around a size ten. They would—of course—have to be measured by the crime scene techs. The other set appears to be about the same size as my shoes were, which will make it easy to eliminate one set immediately. No tread markings on the pair that didn't belong to me. Just the outline of a pointed or tapered-toed shoe. Maybe pointed isn't the correct term. Rounded is probably more accurate, but less so than a pair of sneakers. *Could be deck shoes?* I noted mentally.

Annapolis isn't too far from here. Maybe a cadet strayed from campus for their winter break and found themselves a party to crash. That theory started making sense the second it cropped up in my mind. Only a military trained soldier could get the drop on four suspects, subdue them and kill them so quickly that they couldn't fight back. That, or a ninja. But I haven't seen many of them in the District lately, so I'm going with my first hunch.

Can't rule anything out at this point. Not until we have our IDs. Once we have that, then we can start narrowing down our suspect pool. Until then, everyone on this campus is on my radar.

COLUMBIA HEIGHTS

12:49 PM

When Diamond returned, I filled him in on Davis and Miller being on their lunch break while we were upstairs. He shrugged his shoulders in a "what can we do about it," way. He didn't look too happy when I asked him to head back to the car to radio for backup.

I showed him the ladder first as an incentive to get him to do what I wanted him to do. I can't ask, ask, ask, all the time without giving him a little something in return every now and then. Not if I want him to keep being my gopher, at least.

My nap was already wearing me down. Trying to make sense of the killer's escape, I tried to get a read on our location. I'm not all that familiar with this campus. Besides a few trips to the university hospital, this is my first trip onto the campus itself. Looking around, I saw nothing that looked familiar. But, seeing how being in the back alley between a row of houses and a larger faculty building took away my sight lines from the normal street view, it wasn't surprising that I felt lost.

Looking at the footprints in the dust got me thinking. A) I was going to have to get Sarah back out here to snap some photographs, and B) I wondered if we could sneak away for a lunch date.

Probably not. At least not with Cole—the puppy dog—hot on my heels everywhere I go.

It's been a long time since I've had these new-relationship butter-flies in my stomach. Probably not since me and the wife started dating all those years ago.

That ended horribly, and seeing how I royally botched the first attempt with Sarah, I'm trying my hardest to not make the same mistakes again, this time around.

Our second first date went off without a hitch, though. We went to some fancy place downtown. Her choice. Above my pay grade—but I wanted to impress her and to let her know I wasn't the same person I was all those years ago. It must've worked, since she still wants to see me. But she's been pretty adamant that we keep our work lives pro-fessional. So that means a lunch date is probably out of the question.

Off in the distance, I could see the steeple that Howard University was known for. I wondered if that would be where the administration offices were. Probably a safe bet. We would most likely fare better with walking, I thought. I've heard that parking was an issue on this campus, not that it would matter since it's Christmas break and all. Plus, walking would give us a chance to look for any more blood drippings or any other clues that might lead us to the identity of the killer and how he escaped.

The perk of having Cole as a partner is the fact that I can stretch the legs out from time to time. 'Ol Jackie Boy was keen on driving everywhere we went, even if it was only across the street.

Lost in thought while staring at the impressive architecture of the main building, I heard footsteps coming up behind me. I turned to see Cole about fifty yards away. I hadn't even realized I had walked that far away from the ladder. And here I was pissed that Davis and Miller left the crime scene unattended. Now I was guilty of doing the same thing.

"McFweed is on his way now," the kid told me. "He's gonna put in a call to the crime scene technician as well. They'll snap their photos and haul the ladder back in for processing for us."

I nodded in agreement. Half listening, half still lost in thought with the majestic steeple in my view.

Ted McFweed was the homicide lieutenant on our shift. He has a reputation around the precinct of being a goody-two-shoes, which resulted in many of the officers calling him "Teed McFweed" behind his back. I was guilty of it from time to time too, though I tried to take the high road around the man. We've kind of got a history. Though over the years it has mellowed a bit, there is definitely still some tension between us on most days. We can now actively work a case together without getting overly heated with one another, at least.

"Good," I replied. "You see that building over there? The one with the steeple?" I asked him while pointing towards the main campus.

"Yeah, what about it?"

"I'm guessing that's where the administration offices are, so once backup arrives, we should probably head over there. Maybe we can get a clue as to who lived in the house here. We don't have time to wait for the positive IDs, and this way we can at least start building a suspect pool. Even if we have to amend it later."

"You're the boss, Max. Just point me in the right direction."

I let his comment slide and followed Diamond back toward the gate that led to the backyard of the house. I was getting hot, and I didn't like it. Not quite the bad temper kind of hot, but close. I just hated waiting, to be honest. Impatience isn't my most redeeming quality, especially now while I'm trying my best not to drink in circumstances when I normally would have. This definitely counted as one of those times.

It was an unusually sunny afternoon for the end of December—especially after the freak snowstorm we just had—and the sunlight hitting my dark jacket was making me sweat. Not that I'm complaining. I'd much rather have some heat hit the side of my face than the normal rain drops or sleet of the season, but it was still getting my nerves up. Knowing we still probably had thirty minutes to kill before McFweed and company showed up, I was beginning to feel claustrophobic. Even though we were standing outside in the alley.

I've never been one for small talk, but especially not when it's with someone I didn't know all that well. Like I said before, Diamond and I have only worked together for a couple of months. If we weren't talking about a case, we had nothing else to talk about. Normally I would bring up the 'Skins in a situation like this, but after their abysmal 3-9 season, I'd rather sit in quiet than talk about that mess.

Besides, football was just something to occupy my time until baseball season rolled around again. Not that my Senators put forth much more of an effort than their football counterparts, finishing dead last in the league with only 50 wins to their 104 losses. I shook my head at that thought and put it behind me. No sense getting worked up over something as silly as grown men playing a child's game. There was a time when I lived and died by how the Senators did but seems like I replaced that with the bottle somehow over the years.

And I already knew about Cole's past, anyway; how he aced his detective's exam after his partner was gunned down during what should have been a routine traffic stop. And honestly, after losing my own partner just two months earlier, I knew how deep that wound cut, so I didn't really want him to relive that pain any more than necessary. Though Jack was still alive, I was still having a hard time adjusting to this new situation.

I still rang him on the telephone regularly. Jack, that is. Often bouncing ideas off of him when they arose on a case. I knew he didn't mind. Kept his mind fresh. And it gave him some sense of importance, too.

He wasn't exactly thrilled by taking leave from the badge, but sometimes things just aren't up to us. Old age catches up to all of us at one point or another. His just happened to come while I was still in the prime of mine. No fault of anyone there. Just circumstances that were out of our control.

My inner dialogue continued on with little regard to what was happening around me as I watched Diamond with astonishment. *He really has no clue.* Sure, a promotion is always good, but sometimes—if it comes prematurely—it can backfire in an instant. I guess that's why he was partnered with me. Seeing as how I was now one of the senior detectives in the Metropolitan Police Department, I guess the brass thought I could keep him on the straight and narrow. The jury is still out on that process, but I like to think we are learning from each other. *There I go getting all philosophical again*, I thought to myself with a chuckle.

I could hear footsteps coming around the far side of the house as we reentered into the backyard of the property, snapping me back to reality. *Thank god.* I really didn't want to give McFweed any ammo for me not being on top of my game. Not now, at least. Not while I'm already annoyed by the elusiveness of this unknown killer.

"Show me what you got," McFweed said, as he finally came around the corner of the house.

"Back here," I responded with a point to the alley. "Looks like the killer made his way to the second-story window via a ladder we found out there."

I pointed out the blood droplets in the grass on our way back out to the alley. Officer Barros—who had accompanied McFweed—dropped a yellow numbered cone at each drop. Signaling where we wanted Sarah to snap her photographs.

As we passed through the gate, I stopped and pointed towards the ladder. "There," I said. "That's the one."

COLUMBIA HEIGHTS
December 20th, 7:04 PM

"No! No! No!" Jimmy screamed at the sight of the four bodies on the living room floor, possibly alerting the entire neighborhood to his presence in the house. The horror scene that bore out in front of him was too much as he nearly lost his supper. Quick thinking brought both of his hands to his mouth as he once again swallowed the rancid contents of his stomach.

This wasn't how this was supposed to play out. Yes, he had planned on robbing his girlfriend of her most prized possession, but that was all. There was no killing involved in his plan. This was bad. He had to get out of there.

Tears instantly filled his eyes as he fumbled with the door handle, trying with all of his might to escape the horrors that were filling up his vision. Slamming the door behind him, he took four steps at a time as he bound down the stairs with the speed of a cat being chased by a dog.

Once out of the house, his pace never slowed. Not until he found Boyd in the getaway car three blocks away—engine idling—awaiting his friend and their ticket out of poverty. Not only was their plan never going to come to fruition, but now they had a whole new slew of worries to bring them down as well.

"Where's the card?" Boyd asked. Wondering why it looked like his friend had tears running down his face. "I wanna hold it in my hands just once before we hock it."

"They're dead, Boyd. All of them," Jimmy blurted out as his body limply folded into the car. His voice was as empty as his gaze. Not offering any sort of explanation, he soon added in a shaky voice, "we need to get to a pay phone."

"What're you talking about, Jimmy? Who's dead?"

"Ruby-Sue, Becca, Stella, Deja. All of them. Dead!" Jimmy couldn't fathom what was coming out of his mouth as he stared straight ahead through the car's window, oblivious to his friend's words. It was like he awoke from a nightmare right there in his buddy's car. But this reality was no dream. "They were lying in pools of blood on Ruby-Sue's living room floor. There was so much blood, Boyd. Everywhere you looked, there was blood."

The sound of rubber squealing on asphalt permeated into the quiet night as Boyd hit the gas and tore out of his parking spot. Alerting the ears of all the unsuspecting citizens of that part of town that there was some sort of ruckus going on.

Not fully understanding what his friend was saying, Boyd asked, "did they find out you took the card, and that's why you killed them?"

Jimmy said nothing to this. His eyes kept on the road in front of them, scanning their surroundings at a million miles per hour. His face gave away nothing. Only a blank, motionless stare. But his eyes gave away the fact that his brain was churning at a breakneck pace.

Boyd tried again, with the same result. He was more confused now than ever, but he knew his directive.

At last, there was a pay phone up ahead. As he slowed to a stop, Jimmy burst out through the door and ran towards it without saying a word. Boyd stared at him in wonder. Asking himself if he should make a run for it or stay where he was. Wondering if he was an accessory to murder now as well as theft. That was enough to make the decision for him. Without even realizing it until after the fact, Boyd left his friend in the dust. Making his way back home.

He needed to think.

HOWARD UNIVERSITY
December 21st, 1:21 PM

We left McFweed and company with the ladder in the alley as we headed off towards the admissions office. They were going to have their work cut out for them. No need for us to stand around and watch while we had our own work to do.

Neither Sarah nor the rest of the crime scene technicians had arrived yet. Probably better that we didn't wait around. For one thing, I didn't know what hours the admissions office would hold during the holiday break, and another, if I saw Sarah, my mind would only be on her. And there was far too much work to get done for me to be lost in clouded daydreams. I needed to be free and clear in my head to get the most out of this questioning session.

The walk to the admissions building was a lot longer than I realized it would be. Mainly because we kept getting turned around in the maze that was the campus layout. We probably would've been better to go back out to the street and follow the layout of the city roads. Following those sidewalks would've been easier than this mess of concrete that we were currently trying to navigate. We finally ended up cutting through the grass that hugged the building that we were needing to get around, creating our own path through the campus courtyard.

I stopped outside the door to catch my breath. Well, who are we kidding? I stopped to make sure the kid and I were on the same page. I'm still not certain that he retains any of the information that I give him. "Alright, now please tell me you remember what I told you before. About what to look for when I'm questioning a witness?"

"Yeah, yeah. I got it. Sit and be seen, not heard. Watch for tells, and report to you if their body language raises any red flags. I got it," he said with a tinge of sarcasm. "You got the zorros or something, Max?"

"No, I ain't got the god damn zorros, Cole, it's just, something in my gut says we need to pay attention in there today. Don't know what it is, but I gots me a feeling." Truth was, I was still a bit miffed at having to wait for McFweed to show up back in the alley, but I wasn't going to let the kid know that. Man, I needed a drink in the worst way.

"Okay, okay. No need to bite my head off. I know the routine. You ain't gots to bring it up every time we ask some folks some questions."

"Just keep an eye on them, will ya?" I said with more than an ounce of annoyance in my voice.

"Gotcha, Max. Sorry to ruffle your feathers," he retorted, as his entire face was showing his discomfort. Seems he can dish it out just fine. He just has a problem when it comes back at him.

Other than getting his newfound attitude in check, one of the things I have been working on with Cole is his ability to read people. When you're a uniformed officer, you're asked to read the severity of the situation quickly by examining your perpetrator's body language and assessing the amount of danger you may or may not face while you approach them.

But as a detective, it is completely different. Most of the time, a questioning session comes in a controlled situation. Often in the confines of a room that we're in charge of. Other times, like the one we were about to enter, it comes at a place where the person we are questioning is already comfortable in. So it is very important to get a read on their body language. Especially when it is someone that we don't think is actually on our radar, but rather one that we are trying to gather information from. There should be no reason for that person to be alarmed or act guilty when we're asking for general information, but more often than not, the badge turns even the most innocent of people into someone who looks like they're hiding a closet full of dead bodies.

As I approached the front doors to the giant red-brick steepled building, Diamond followed a few paces behind me. He was staring up at the clock tower in awe, not really paying much attention to where his feet were going. He still didn't have the confidence of a seasoned detective and it showed clear as day as his gait was one of a drunken sailor at the moment. Which was another of the reasons I elected for him to be the observer more often than not. He wasn't likely to ruin anything, but, for now, I thought it was still best for him to keep watch from afar and get the details that I couldn't focus on while asking the questions.

"Hello, ma'am," I said as I fished my tin out of the inside pocket of my jacket as we entered the building. A college aged girl stood at attention behind a darkened wood-colored countertop as we walked in through the door. The room seemed to be not at all like what I had expected from the outside. It was filled with modern furniture you might expect to see at a fancy new hotel downtown, not a hundred-year-old building of higher education. The cushioned chairs, with their lime green throw pillows, really knocked me for a loop.

Though inviting, it was probably the last thing I expected to see this morning.

"I'm Detective Max Denver with the Metropolitan Police Department," I said, taking control of the situation. "This here is my partner, Cole Diamond. We are looking into the murders that took place on campus last evening."

"Such a tragic thing, isn't it? I knew the two girls who lived in that house. We had a class together. They were always so happy, it seemed. I just can't imagine who would do such a thing." Her face turned away as she was trying to hide the fact that tears had welled up in her eyes.

As she reached for a tissue from a box on the counter, I asked, "so you knew them? Sorry to be so blunt about this, but you think you could give me their names? We haven't had any luck with IDs on any of them yet."

Through a few sniffles, she gave us what we were after. "The two girls that lived in the house were Ruby-Sue Daniels and Deja Moore." Another round of sobbing followed. I looked back toward Diamond—who was sitting in a chair with his notebook out—as the room suddenly filled with a silence too uncomfortable for my liking. Something about watching a woman cry always makes me feel uneasy.

"I heard there were four girls in total that were found last night. I only know of the two that lived there though," she continued while trying to stifle more sobs. She must've picked up on my unease because she answered my next question without my prompting her. "But my guess is the other two girls were Becca Wainwright and Stella Peters. The four of them were thick as thieves they were. Never did anything alone. Always went out together and stayed pretty close to their little group."

Once again, I diverted my look from the girl to Diamond. This time, making sure the kid was doing his job and writing the names down into his notebook. He was. Not that I'm handing out gold stars or anything, but it's nice to know that what I've been teaching him is actually sticking.

"What about any boyfriends or anything?" I asked. "From the looks of things, the house served as something of a party destination on campus."

"You're not wrong about that, but I think most of the partying came from the occupants downstairs. Both Ruby-Sue and Deja were all about academia. Grades were very important to both of them." The tears seemed to subside for the time being, which was a relief to me. "Not to say they didn't have their fun. They weren't squares. Not in the least bit. College kids are going to party, but those girls had their heads in the books for the most part."

I thought it was odd that she skipped over my last question, so I pressed her with it again. "And any boyfriends? Or anybody you think we should be keen on?"

"Ruby-Sue did have a boyfriend. Some punk who isn't a student here. I don't know what she saw in him honestly, but he came along shortly after her spilt with her ex. His name is Jimmy. I don't know him all that well, but I don't like him. I don't trust him as far as I could throw him. He's bad news. Him and his sidekick, too. Kid named Boyd. He seems a little off, but I don't know what it is about either of them. I just don't like them."

"Thank you, miss," I started, but realized I never got her name.

"Watson. Emily Watson." It appears that she's got this mind reading thing down. Maybe I should ask her for some pointers. Sure would make our job a hell of a lot easier.

"Well, thank you Miss Watson. Do you know the last name of Jimmy, by any chance?"

"No, I'm sorry I don't. I only met him once or twice. Like I said, I didn't like the guy. I didn't want to be any more chummy than I had to be with him."

"Okay, not a problem. You've been a lot of help. Thank you for your time." I reached back into my inside jacket pocket and fished out a card with our names and the station phone number on it. "If you can think of anything else, please give us a call," I said while handing her the card.

"I will. Most certainly."

"Oh, and one more thing," I added as I turned for the door. "Do you have a name for this ex-boyfriend of Ruby-Sue's?"

"No, I'm afraid I don't. She kept him pretty secret from the rest of us. Not that she was ashamed of him or anything, but there was something about the way she spoke about him that made the rest of us know not to ask too much. I never even saw him, never once met him. He was just some mystery guy to the rest of us. But she seemed happy, so I never bugged her about any details about the guy."

"What exactly do you mean by that? In what way did she speak of him? How did you know not to ask too many questions?" Diamond asked from out of nowhere. I gave him a quick look before realizing that they were actually excellent questions. Maybe he's right and I am too hard on him. I'll have to remember to give him a few more inches' length the next time we question someone.

"Just that she didn't seem to ever want to discuss the specifics of what he did for a living or even where they met. That sort of thing. I mean, in all honesty, to hear her tell it, she made him sound like the second coming of Christ. But she made it adamantly clear that she didn't want to discuss anything about his personal life at all. Including even something as simple as his name."

"Didn't that seem suspicious to you? I mean, if Cole here started dating some new broad and wouldn't tell me her name, I'd be getting whiplash from all the red flags I'd be dodging."

She gave a little laugh before answering, "at first, yeah, sure. But after seeing how happy she was, I figured she'd just tell me who he was when she felt it was the right time. And then they broke up," she said as she looked at the ceiling behind me. As if pondering if she had missed any warning signs that her friend had inadvertently shown her.

"Do you know why they split?" I asked out of curiosity mainly, but also to see if there was any animosity involved that could warrant a question of motive.

"You know, I'm not really sure," she explained. "She seemed so happy, then one day she said they broke up. It was completely out of the blue. The next thing I knew, Jimmy was in her life. This all happened within the last few weeks. Right about the time we were having our end of the semester final exams. I'm sure more of the story would've come out," she broke off with a sigh. "I guess we'll never know now."

"Okay, thank you for that information. Once again, we appreciate you giving us the time. You've given us a lot to go on. You've got a way to reach us on that card there. Please don't hesitate to get in touch. Even if it's something you don't think is that big of a deal."

She nodded in agreement as I headed for the door. Diamond flipped his notepad shut and was up from his chair and on my heels in no time, almost like there was some sort of transparent tether attached to the both of us.

"So whatcha think here, Max?" He asked once we were walking back towards the front door.

"I think we gots a name we need to track down. That's what I think," I said with purpose. "Maybe this Jimmy fella can tell us what was in that picture frame that was so damn valuable that it warranted the killing of four girls. Notice anything in her body language that I should know about?"

"No, not really. Other than her pauses to wipe the tears away, she seemed as normal as a person could, seeing as this ain't the greatest situation to be in."

"That's what I got out of it, too. Good work, kid." I looked back at him just as the grin on his face faded.

As we were walking out, and man of no more than thirty years of age entered the door as I held it open. He carried a briefcase, but didn't necessarily have the look of either a college professor or a student. "Gentlemen," he said as he passed by. Normally this would be odd, but for where we were at the moment, it didn't surprise me one bit. We were the two that were out of place on this campus, not him. Still, no matter where the instance took place, if I had been seen by any of my coworkers holding a door open for a colored man, I would've been reprimanded on the spot.

"Detectives," I heard Miss Watson call out before the doors closed all the way. "This is Mr. Embry," she said as she tugged on the arm of the man with the briefcase, turning him to face us as we too had turned our direction and started back inside the building. "He's the TA in the class I took with Ruby-Sue and Deja. He worked pretty closely with both of them on their term papers."

I reached into the inside pocket of my jacket and fished out another card to hand him. "Unfortunately, Mr. Embry, we are running short on time at the moment. Miss Watson can probably fill you in on the questions we are concerned with, and if anything comes up or if there's something more you think we should know, call us, please."

"Will do," he said as he turned and headed down the hallway. Before he got too far, he once again turned and asked us another question.

"Do you gentlemen have any leads yet? Do you know who it was that did this?"

"Unfortunately, no," I replied. "That's why we're here today. We now have names to go off of though, so we will be diving deep into the lives of each and every family member and associate of the four girls. We'll get it figured out. Don't you worry about that."

He nodded at my response before turning back down the hall. Maybe it was the grief of losing a few of his students—I couldn't figure it out—but whatever reasoning he had, he didn't seem to be too keen on sticking around and talking with us. Fine by me. We had a couple of people to seek out, anyway. Can't waste a whole day of work in this office today.

"What gives, Max? Shouldn't we be questioning him as well? Seems like he knew the girls fairly well," Diamond asked.

"We've already got two names to track down, Cole. What he tells us probably won't amount to any new information. Best to not waste our time on that right now."

Not that Diamond was wrong in his assessment of Mr. Embry, but we had suspects in our sights already. No need to waste energy on something that would not get us any closer to solving these murders. I took notice of his pace and added, "but write down his name in your notebook just in case. We may need to track him down again in the future."

BROOKLAND, WASHINGTON D.C.

December 22nd, 12:58 AM

He packed his bags in a hurry and tossed them into the trunk of his car. Not worrying where, or how, they came to land. They were just clothes. Nothing of value there. He had his prize on him, wrapped in cardboard in the pocket of his jacket to keep it safe. Any wrinkles or creases would bring its value down substantially.

That was the only thing on his mind at that moment. Well, that, and the fact that he was sure the cops were onto him, too. Though he couldn't figure out where that paranoia was coming from. He knew that he had stayed hidden in the alley, waiting until the flashlights had extinguished before he pulled away. Besides, it was too dark back there for anybody to get a good read on his car, anyway. Or at least that's what he hoped was the case.

He knew it was stupid to go back to the crime scene, but his intuition led him there, anyway. Call it guilt for what he had done, or maybe even curiosity to see what the police were looking for at the crime scene. Regardless, he knew it was a boneheaded move to put himself that close to the crosshairs of the fuzz.

As he tried to hide in the shadows outside of his house, he frantically looked in all directions, making sure nobody spotted him. Despite the near-freezing temperatures, sweat was beading on his brow. His nerves were getting the best of him.

It was after midnight, and the neighborhood was quiet. Yet he was still as spooked as a kid in a haunted house. Jumping at every noise he heard, thinking his run towards freedom was coming to an end before it even got started.

He planned on only being gone for one night, but who knew if the heat had been turned up on him or not? He hadn't heard of any suspects from the murders yet. Still, he packed enough clothes for one week, just in case. Suspicion was running high. He felt he shouldn't stick around and wait for the cops to put two and two together.

The streetlights illuminated his vehicle as if it were under a spotlight on a stage. Giving him the fear that he was under a spotlight himself. But this wasn't stage fright he was feeling. A line had been crossed, and he had no idea how to get back on the right side of it.

First things first. He had to unload the merchandise. Which was where he was off to at close to one in the morning in the late December darkness.

No stolen loot equals no motive for murder. That's what he was telling himself, at least.

He had a meeting with a guy he had looked up in the yellow pages. A man who specialized in sports memorabilia. He was going to unload his prize and collect his booty. Only problem was, he had to meet him in Baltimore by 7 A.M. Which was why he was leaving in the middle of the night.

He knew he had been careful. Besides, with how much time he had spent with Ruby-Sue, his fingerprints were bound to be found somewhere over there. And that was easy enough to explain away.

He would probably lose his job over this once their relationship hit the news. But that beat doing a span in Lorton.

He could find another job. But what he couldn't do was replace his life if they took away his freedom from him. If he had to run for the rest of his life, that's what he was willing to do. And that would be a lot easier now with the money he would be fetching in the morning. If everything went according to plan, that is.

$10,000 could easily get him into Canada. Hell, he could even try to disappear into Europe if he wanted to. It was the 1950s, after all. A black man in England wasn't as farfetched as it once was. He could learn the accent and assimilate into a new life easily enough. There were bound to be plenty of places to hide out in. Small towns he could disappear in, anonymous jobs to take, etcetera.

The only thing he had left to lose was now dead after she left him for that punk kid. No, his life as he knew it before was gone, anyway. No reason to come back here.

He shut his car door as quietly as he could while he climbed behind the steering wheel. He took one last long look at his home—taking in all the memories he had accumulated throughout the years—knowing that this was most likely the last time he would ever see it again. He wiped a tear from his cheek as he said a final silent goodbye before driving off into the darkness.

COLUMBIA HEIGHTS
December 21st, 1:59 PM

We watched the crime scene van pull away as we neared the alley. McFweed was still there shooting the shit with Officer Barros, as if they were waiting for us to return to fill them in on our meeting. Made sense, though. Why wait until we filled out our reports at the end of our shift when they could get the information they needed right now?

Daniel Barros, an eleven-year vet with Metro PD, seems to have become McFweed's new lapdog recently. Every lieutenant has one, and if they're lucky, they will be as loyal as an actual dog. I've never had a problem with the guy, but you know what they say about the company that you keep. Suffice it to say, the look we got from Barros was less than cordial as we walked back toward the area of the ladder.

"Whatcha find out?" McFweed asked once we were within earshot. Barros stood at attention as if all of a sudden he seconded that question.

"Got two names. Ruby-Sue Daniels and Deja Moore. Those were the two girls that lived here," I said as I pointed over towards the house. "The two other girls aren't a positive, but according to the girl from admissions, the other two are most likely Becca Wainwright and Stella Peters. The way she told it, the four of them were pretty much inseparable."

"Also, gots two names of interest for us to track down and question," I continued. "Well, first names only, but this girl didn't speak too highly of them. Names are Jimmy and Boyd. Neither of them are students here at Howard. Don't know their age, but this Jimmy kid was dating Daniels. Oh, and there's another guy we need to get a hold of too somehow. Used to date Daniels but turns out nobody knows his name. Go figure."

"Well, it's a start," McFweed said in response. "Once I get back to the station, I'll try to get a hold of next of kin. I'm betting they live out of state, so it might be a few days before we can get positive IDs. Maybe the folks of the two that lived here can give us some insight into the two Jane Doe's. Good job, boys. See you back at the office."

I looked at McFweed with eyes as big as saucers. He has never even come close to complimenting me before and I was a bit taken aback by it. Crazy bastard was full of surprises.

Before McFweed could add anything negative and ruin my good mood, I gave Diamond a nod and started back towards our car. I knew he would not like this, but I had to get on the phone.

Only one man I knew that could shake out a ghost in an early morning fog.

Jack Barnaby.

MPD MID-TOWN PRECINCT

December 21st, 2:15 PM

Once we were back at the precinct, the first thing I did was pick up the receiver of my desk phone and dial a number that I knew by heart. While the call was going through, I combed over the paperwork that had been left on my desk since the last time I sat at it. Jack answered on the second ring.

"J and N Investigations, Jack speaking," he said through the telephone in a gruff but sincere voice.

After his retirement from the department, he got into the private sector, naming his company J and N, naturally. The N was for his late beloved wife, Nettie. The J was for, of course, Jack. He took mostly lost pets and cheating spouse cases. Nothing too over the top or anything he would have to exude too much energy on. Mainly he did it just to give himself something to do. He wasn't ready to hang up his cuffs yet, but at his age, it was the right thing to do. The pension that came along with it wasn't too shabby, either.

"Jackie Boy. How goes it, buddy-ol-pal," I returned, not wanting to make it known that this call was for a favor. Even though I know he knew better. Over half of the calls I've made to him since he retired have been for help on a case I'm working.

"Maxey, good to hear your voice. Whatcha gots for me this time?" He knew me all too well.

"I do need some help, Jackie Boy. You got me there," I responded with a laugh. "This guy we need to track down seems to be a ghost. The young gal over at the Howard University admissions office brought him up. Don't know if he's involved or not, but my senses started tingling when she mentioned him," I explained.

"You caught that mess from last night, did ya?" The tone of his voice sounded both painful and optimistic. He was always glad to help me out, as it gave him a sense of being back at it, but I knew deep down that it hurt him at the same time. Especially knowing that he wouldn't get credit for any of the collars that they credited Diamond and I for. At least not officially. "I heard it over the radio as I was turning in for bed. Kept me up half the night thinking about them poor girls. Shame what this world is coming to."

Though he was officially retired, he told me he kept an ear on the radios. He was still having a hard time learning how to officially switch off from working man to retiree. I don't blame him. Retirement is something that I don't want to think about for a long time. Even though this job has brought out the worst in me at times, it's still who I am. I don't want to think about what I would become without that badge in my pocket. Especially now, as I'm trying my damndest to dry out once and for all. The tin was all I had as a reminder of who I was. What my life's calling is.

"Yup. Me and Diamond were at the house until well after midnight last night. Still no positives on any of the four of them yet, but we think we at least have two names to go on now. Just have to track down next of kin to get that confirmation."

It's hard for me to not spill my guts and tell him everything I know. He was the lone person I could lean on for over half of my career. I told the man everything—and I do mean everything—whether or not he wanted to hear it. But I can't do that anymore. I'm slowly learning that I have to draw a line in the sand when it comes to giving him all the information we have. Even if I know he can help us. Not that I don't want to fill him in on our cases, but it's department protocol. We're not supposed to share too much with civilians. Ex partners or not.

"Turns out, one girl had a previous boyfriend that I think we should get in contact with," I continued. "Only thing is, we don't know a damn thing about him. Seems like nobody does. No name, no age, no place of work. Nothin."

Hearing the frustration in my voice, he said, "give me the girl's name, and I'll see what I can dig up."

"Thanks, Jack, you're a lifesaver."

I gave him the names of both of the girls that we assume lived at the house and I hung up the phone. Now I had to deal with the sulking puppy dog that was my partner.

I swear, every time I bring up the name Jack Barnaby, it sets him off into one of his moods. When we worked together for the first time, he showed the confidence of a seasoned vet—even giving me an ultimatum in the car after I was a few too many sips deep. But now that he's my partner, any time I disagree with him, he acts like he's being sent back down to the minors or something. Never giving me attitude or anything, he just sulks like a tiny little puppy dog.

I sighed deep. Exhaling out all the anger that was suddenly filling up in my brain as I looked across my desk at my partner. It wasn't hate filled; I don't think. More like frustration. I sometimes forget that he has big shoes to fill, which is probably even harder than my job of showing him the ropes. Regardless, the sigh was loud enough that a few of the other detectives looked up from their paperwork at me. They all knew what was coming. The sound even made one of them hastily retreat to the head before the inevitable ensuing eruption came. I know the look that Cole was giving me and frankly; I didn't have enough alcohol on me to deal with it properly.

While stacking the papers on my desk in a neat pile to help me focus, I took two more deep breaths. I was trying my damndest to keep my composure before dealing with what I knew was going to get me heated.

"Don't you even start with me, Cole," I said as I got up from my desk. The redness of my face was apparent from the sweat that started beading up around the collar of my shirt.

"You know as well as I do, Barnaby can use his knowledge to get us that name easier than we can," I explained in a voice that was a tad on the loud side. "Plus, while he's out doing that, we can run down the two guys we have names for. Don't think of it as I trust him more than you. Think of it as he's doing us a favor while we don't have the time to do it ourselves."

I took a few paces towards him, thinking he would slink farther into his seat. But what came next, I think surprised everyone in the station.

"You're right, Max, I second guess myself every step of the way. I know I'm here before I should be and worry that everybody else thinks the same thing," he started to say before I stopped him.

"Let me just stop you right there, pal. To be honest, there's not one person in this precinct that thinks you're ready for this," I said as I laid it on pretty thick as he stood up and was now face to face with me. I did not mean my statement to be scolding in any way, but more of a confidence building lesson. "Well, maybe one, McFweed, but other than that, you're right. Nobody believes you should be in plain clothes. You're young. You're green. You lack confidence. But you know what changes that?"

"What's that?" He asked, not once cowering. His face was still about a fist's length away from mine.

"Stop with the woe-is-me bullshit and get your job done," I said, as my voice rose even more. "Come up with a plan. Execute that plan and solve the damn murder. You think they handed me my gold shield on a platter and gave me the keys to the city? Hell no! I was right where you are. Now cut the crap, grow a pair, and let's get to work. You're already a step above where I was at your age. So I want you to dig deep into your gut, or whatever you need to do, and find the man that told me he was gonna run up the ladder and rat me out if my drinking got in the way again. Now that was a man of character. One of virtue. One that I would be proud to call a partner. Find that man again, and not one person around this joint will ever second guess you again. You hear what I'm saying, Cole?"

"Loud and clear," he said with a puffed-up chest and as much gusto of a cadet being screamed at by a drill sergeant. "You're right, Max. They chose me to do this job for a reason. Whether or not I think I'm ready, Ted does. And I can't let him down."

"That's more like it. Okay, now that that's out of the way, it's time to prove it. Prove to me you deserve an extra length of freedom on that imaginary leash I have around your neck. You do that, and I promise you I'll let you lead the questioning when I think you're ready."

"Thanks, Max."

"Don't thank me yet. You still haven't proven you can put your own damn shoes on by yourself. Do, don't say. Show, don't tell. Get my drift?"

"Yes," he said with confidence as he followed in behind me.

"Okay, now go ask McFweed to run down some IDs that fit the names and ages of our two guys, Jimmy and Boyd."

"Roger that," he said as he trotted out of the bullpen and up to the lieutenant's desk by the front door.

I hadn't realized how much my little pep talk had gotten me heated. My voice had raised more than a few decibels, and half the department was staring at me as I grabbed my jacket and started heading back out the door behind Diamond.

The look of awe was on nearly everyone's faces. I ignored them all and focused on the door straight ahead. No point in giving them what they wanted. Can't be a hard-ass if I stopped to receive a standing ovation every time I said something meaningful. I had big shoes to fill. Jack Barnaby never took a second to bask in glory, and neither would I. Not when I was tasked at bringing the next great Metropolitan Homicide detective up.

I was past McFweed's desk and halfway through the front door of the precinct by the time Diamond realized I was leaving and finally caught up.

"Where we going?" He asked with shortened breath.

"To go see Frank Allcott at the morgue. See if my hunch is correct. Then we have a couple of names to track down."

CITY Morgue, Washington D.C.

December 21st, 3:15 PM

F rank had four tables in his otherwise nearly bare room as we walked in through the swinging double doors. Seemed like he was simultaneously working on all four of the girls at once with the blankets draped down to the waist on each victim.

Though the blood had stopped spitting out on its own many hours ago, each table had a red-hued hose leading from the body to the drain in the center of the floor. I could see the knife wounds clear as day from the moment I walked into the room. The organs were so damaged that they were fileted and protruding through the wounds caused by the sharp steel. Spewing the insides onto the clean outer layer of flesh. Not a sight for the squeamish, I'll tell you that much. I probably should've given a warning to Cole, but I figured this should be another learning experience for him. Blood and gore come with the job. If he didn't know that ahead of time, there was nothing I could do to remedy that problem for him now.

Frank looked up from the body he was currently investigating at the sound of the two of us entering. Though I've been in this room more times than I can count, the smell of the antiseptic solution still hits me straight in the back of the throat like a ton of bricks every single time. A quick gasp of air had to be handled professionally. Cole hadn't mastered this technique yet as he turned and ran towards the sink, both hands covering his mouth as we saw the color vanish from his face.

I don't know what was more disturbing. The sight of the four girls in the center of the room—sliced and diced the way that they were—or the sound of my partner losing his lunch behind me. Regardless, Frank, ever the professional that he was, saw my dilemma and came to the rescue. Without missing a beat, he grabbed a clean towel off of the counter, handed it to Cole, and poured a cup of water for him from the tap. Killing two birds with one stone. If there were ever a person to not get sick themselves from cleaning up one's upchuck, it would be Frank. This was like a walk in the park for him after seeing what the cruelty our humanity offers and brings him on a daily basis.

"Sorry about that, Frankie. Seems like I forgot to mention the state these girls might be in to my partner. Won't let it happen again," I said with a slight chuckle. Partly because I was embarrassed, and partly because I actually thought it was funny. We've all been there. It's human instinct to react the way that Diamond did. Just a story to look back on and laugh at in a few years' time. "We're here on a hunch, actually. Just wanted to see if my theory was correct."

"Oh yeah? And what would that be, Maxey?" the examiner asked.

"Back at the house last night, the way the bodies were laid out with the amount of blood there was in the room. It kinda made me believe that this was personal. And that I'd be willing to bet that one of these girls took the brunt of the punishment."

"You gotta secret camera in here somewhere or something, Denver? You nailed that one right on the head. To say she took the brunt would be an understatement," he said as he walked us over to the examination tables in the center of the room.

"Three of the four girls had seven stab or slash marks on them. But this one here," he continued as he directed our attention to the body that was the farthest from where we were standing, "this one here took over forty. Well, I was at number forty when you's two walked in through the doors, at least. That number may be a lot higher by the time I'm done with my investigation. How'd you know?"

"Don't ask me, just something my gut told me. When it speaks, I take out my pencil and start taking notes," I said while laughing.

Cole seemed to be back from his bout of illness as he once again joined me by my side at the sound of my laughter. Kudos to Frank. An autopsy room is by far the least funny room a man can go in, but Frank seems to have a way of making the conversation so casual that you temporarily forget where you're at. Easing the minds of all who enter. I've never been there when he's pulled back the sheet to show a loved one the face of their fallen kin, but I'm sure he handles that even better than he handled Cole's weak stomach.

"So whatcha thinking, then? Jilted lover? Jealousy? Or completely random? I think that about covers it for motives these days, right?" Frank asked with a nervous laugh. He often played this game with us as if he were trying to play amateur sleuth while coming to conclusions about how his victims were murdered.

"Close, but you forgot one," I said with a little less enthusiasm than we all had a moment earlier. "Armed robbery. Of course, it's too early to say that was the cause for these girls' demise, but it appears that there was something missing in one of the bedrooms.

"I'm guessing it was her room," I continued with a point to the girl with most of the knife wounds. "It also sounds like there might have been a love triangle in the midst here as well. Like I said, it's too early to tell. But you know me. I ain't done until I flipped each and every stone over."

"I believe the phrase you're looking for is 'no stone unturned,' Denver."

"See? This is why I like you, Allcott. You can bust 'em like the best of 'em," I said with another laugh.

"But in all seriousness, if I may," I continued, after the laughter in the room died down. "We found a kitchen knife on the floor with the bodies. I'm guessing that was the weapon of choice last night. My question to you is, does it look like any of these girls put up a fight of any kind? The way the bodies were left made it almost look ritualistic. The four of them were laid neatly in a circle around the weapon. And like I said before, blood was everywhere in that room. Everywhere except for the circle in between the four of them where the knife was left. Something isn't sitting right with me about that scene."

"A kitchen knife definitely looks like it would have been what was used. These gashes are deep. There were some minor carving attempts on the three that had minimal damage. But that could've just been because the killer was in a hurry with them. The knife could've just been dragged against their flesh as the killer moved his target. But on the one with most of the wounds, there were no so-called drag marks or carving attempts. Just deep thrusts that nearly penetrated all the way through her body. Which makes me agree with your assessment that it was most definitely personal with her.

"As far as it being a sacrificial killing," Frank continued, "I'm just not seeing anything that supports that theory. For one, no organs are missing from any of the girls. And secondly, like I said before about the drag marks, this was sloppy. There's too much frustration and anger in those knife thrusts for it to be ritualistic. Sacrificial killings are neat and methodical. This was not that. Not in the least."

"Interesting. Well, it was just a hunch. But it makes a lot more sense when you spell it out like that," I said before getting back to one of my previous questions. "Any defensive wounds that you can see? Diamond here thinks maybe they were slipped something that subdued them. Only thing that makes sense for me as to how he got the jump on all four of them. Though, I'm just speculating there. You are planning on doing a toxicology exam too, right?"

"Who do you think we are, Denver. The Army?" Frank asked in a grouchy tone. I must've crossed a line somewhere. He's normally very cordial, but the sneer he put behind that last phrase made me shrink a little. "Yes, of course I'm gonna do a tox screen. That is standard for all autopsies. And as for the defensive wounds, I don't see any, so you may be onto something with them being drugged. I haven't gotten the chance to look under their fingernails yet, but I will take note and put it into my report if there appears to be any skin under any of them. At least then you'll know to be looking for some scratches on your perp's skin."

"Sounds good, Frank. You got an ETA for any of this?"

"No, unfortunately I don't." The attitude was still apparent. Have to make a mental note not to piss him off again in the future. Can't have him twiddling his thumbs on our account when we have killers to catch. "With four bodies, that means there's four times the work for me. But hopefully no later than this time tomorrow. I don't want to rush and miss anything that might be of use to you."

"I appreciate that. Sounds like we're stuck in limbo for the time being then. We'll let you get back to it. Give us a ring when the reports are done. We may not have the liberty of taking our time on this one."

"Will do. Good luck out there, boys. I'll let you know the second I'm done here."

"Thanks, Frank," I said, as I nudged Cole with my elbow and headed back for the double doors. Now came my least favorite part of the job.

Waiting.

ECKINGTON, WASHINGTON D.C.

December 29th, 8:17 PM

From inside the phone booth, Jimmy watched as he saw Boyd peel out and take off. Leaving him behind. He felt like he was all alone for the first time in his life and was wondering what his next move should be.

A long way from home—both physically and mentally—he had no clue as to what he should do. What he even could do. He was numb. Shaking—not because of the cold—but because his body was losing its grip on reality. On the safety of being in control.

At that moment, he had never felt so betrayed or alone in his life. Frightened didn't even come close to describing how out of control he felt. Not even giving a single thought to the irony of the fact that when he had left his home that night, he intended to betray the girl that he told himself he loved.

Not that any of that mattered in the present. Betrayal was a part of Jimmy's life. It was in his blood. Ever since his daddy left him and his mama alone when he was just five years old and instilled that defense mechanism deep into his psyche. But even that long suppressed emptiness paled in comparison to how he felt now as he watched the taillights of Boyd's car fade as they disappeared into the night.

Boyd would come around, he knew that. Or at least deep down he hoped that thought was true. Boyd was easily convinced about most things in life. It was easy to exploit the young man's thoughts. But that didn't help Jimmy now. Not when he needed someone. Someone to help him. Someone to tell him the right thing to do.

Jimmy prided himself on being the leader of the two. But in all honesty, he was just manipulative of a person who was too easy to manipulate. That wasn't leadership. That was authoritarian bullying. He knew it. It's not like he hid that from any of their other friends. It was empowering to have someone at your beck and call to do your dirty work for you.

He couldn't believe Boyd had actually gotten the nerve to think for himself for a change. Not when he really needed him to be the thoughtless drone that he had trained him to be. Leaving him scared and alone and not knowing what to do next. Not being in clear control of every situation was what scared Jimmy the most.

Jimmy slid the heavy wooden phone booth door open as he slowly stepped back out on the sidewalk, contemplating what his next move should be.

The metaphorical angel on his left shoulder told him he should re-enter the phone booth and make the call. Knowing that he was innocent, he had nothing to fear, his conscience told him.

But the Devil on his right shoulder told him to make a run for it. Boyd already didn't believe him—or was too scared to stand by his side—what made him think the cops would believe him? Especially with the regard they gave to colored men. Make that colored men who confessed to planning to rob the house where four girls had been slain.

He took another four steps before stopping again. His brain going back and forth to the pros and cons of his life's greatest choice. He may have not been the most law-abiding citizen in the District up until this point in time, but his mama taught him better than this. Robbing was one thing. That could be forgiven. But letting a murderer walk free was something that Jimmy couldn't live with. Even if it meant alerting the authorities to his own misgivings.

Run, and hope that it didn't come back to haunt him. Can he even be sure that nobody saw him take off out of the house like a man on fire?

Or do the right thing, even with the prospect of not having the police believe his story.

The dilemma was real. So real that he found himself in near convulsions as he fished a dime out of his pocket. Holding the silver disc up to the lamp-lit streetlights, he made his choice.

Inserting the dime into the pay phone's coin slot, he made the call to the operator. No matter the outcome, this was the right thing to do.

MOUNT Vernon square, WASHINGTON D.C.

December 21st, 4:00 PM

"Where we off to now then, Max?" Diamond asked as we were walking back to our car after leaving our meeting with Frank Allcott. He was getting more comfortable with me, but he still wasn't at the point where he thought it was okay to call me "Maxey."

"Back to the shop, I guess," I replied, trying to hide the dejection in my voice. "We got no other leads at the moment. No sense driving around and looking for one. We can at least get a jump on the paperwork that's going to hold us up until the middle of the night."

It's frustrating not having a line of sight on what our next mission is. This would normally be the time I would try to sneak away and put a few shots in me, but I'm trying to be good today. Used to be what I called getting my mind in the game. There's no telling if it worked or not. Even when you're the one who's loaded, it's hard to make out what's up or down when you ask yourself the hard questions. But my hunches seem to be a little on the tamer side of life now without the sauce adding to my exaggerated bravado, though. So, I must be doing something right.

I guess for now I'll sit and stare out the window at the scenery as it passes by, thankful for the fact that I'm not the one driving. The city looks even more depressing while sober. I don't know how Jack did it, getting lost in thought while trying to navigate the streets at the same time. I pondered that thought as I grabbed a stick of spearmint out of my pocket. My new go to for when I crave a nip of the bottle. I couldn't even focus on the road ahead of us as I was searching the depths of my brain for any information that we had gathered that might point us in the right direction.

What did we actually even have?

For starters, two God's honest people to track down, which hopefully won't be as tough as I'm expecting it to be.

It's probably way too early to start compiling a list anyway, but we have to start somewhere. Without a clear-cut lead to direct us in a certain direction, my mind got to work.

Besides the mystery man and the current boyfriend, we have a can of beer in the trash bag that Diamond collected from the crime scene that may or may not lead us anywhere. A photograph from the school newspaper that might tell us who lived in the house, though we pretty much already have our identification on the girls. Some prints that were hopefully collected around the window ledge, picture frame and on the murder weapon. And really, not much else.

But the photograph got my mind going in a new direction. One that my gut alerted me was a good one. I picked up the receiver of the radio from the dash and sent a call into McFweed, hoping that he and

Barros were back from the crime scene by now. I had an idea that might speed up the identification process.

"McFweed here," the scratchy voice through our dash radio said.

"Yeah, Ted, this is Max. We just finished our interview with Allcott, and it got me thinking. Universities issue ID cards to all of their students, which means they will have photographs on record of the four victims. Think we can get Sarah to bring the crime scene photos by the administration office and see if we can't get any positive identification that way?"

"I would normally say no, but seeing as how they probably all were from out of town, this might not be a bad idea. Of course, we'll still have to bring the next of kin in to formally identify each of them. This could definitely help us in not only reaching out to the next of kin, but it also could jumpstart this investigation, too. Good thinking, Max. I'll put a call in to the crime scene office now."

"Roger that, Ted. Denver out," I said as I hung the receiver back into its cradle on the dash.

For the second time in a few hours, the man had complimented me. *What on earth was going on?*

A trace of a smirk showed itself as I turned towards the side window of the car. I couldn't let Diamond see my smile. I had a tough-guy image to uphold. A smile here or a smirk there and he would start to think I was the softy that I try my best to keep under the exterior. Maybe after we work together for a few years, I'll clue him in on the fact that it's all a façade. But for now, his entry to that club is revoked.

It might not be much, but it was a start. Getting official IDs of those girls could really get us heading in the right direction. Could help us track down people who knew the girls, which might give us the last names of Jimmy and Boyd. Who might actually know the name of our mystery man. If everything goes as planned, at least.

Everything is riding on the identities of those four girls. Why wait three to four days to get a hold of family and get them into town when we could go to the school to get what we needed? Seemed like a no-brainer to me. But there always seems to be some bureaucratic nonsense that holds up the easy way to do things.

Which is why I'm just fine being a detective. It's frustrating enough being told no, but I think I would lose my mind if I was stuck playing by all the rules that the boys upstairs were held to. Out on the street, I could bend those rules from time to time to get what I needed. And that was okay by me. What did it really matter if I was bringing a killer to justice? No harm, no foul, if you asked me.

Feeling satisfied that we were finally on the right track, and with nothing else to do but wait, I sat back on my side of the bench seat and relaxed for the first time all day. Taking in all the sights and sounds of our magnificent city. Funny how your outlook on things can change so quickly.

We had Jack working his magic on the fella with no name, and soon Sarah and her team would be at the administration office with their photos.

Seemed to me that me and Cole might actually get to knock off early for a change. Well, if we get a head start on our paperwork, that is.

MPD MID-TOWN PRECINCT

December 21st, 4:41 PM

A fresh new stack of paperwork greeted me as I plopped down onto the chair at my desk. I half-heartedly sifted through them, looking for something that might catch my eye, not really ready for the boring portion of my day to begin yet.

I'd much rather be out on the streets hunting down clues or giving people of interest the business in the form of some tough questions. Maybe even getting a little physical if someone was giving me the runaround. That was a better use of the taxpayer's dollar, in my opinion. I make a difference out there, not at my desk poring over mounds of paperwork. But it was still a part of the job whether I liked it or not. And better to be doing it now around supper time than well into the early morning hours when I could be at home sleeping instead.

I looked across my desk at Diamond's to see if I could get a read on his face. See if anything of note found its way onto his desk as I reshuffled my stack to start from the top again.

His face was one of an expert poker player. But that didn't really tell me anything. Jack had a face that was easy to read. I could tell what he was about to say before the words even came out of his mouth. But with Cole, it was different. Could be that he was just too afraid to make the wrong move, so he kept his face and emotions as guarded as he could. Or maybe he really was just that good. I still hadn't figured it out yet. All I did know was the kid seemed too aloof to score as high as he did on his detective's exam.

The strangest part to me about all of it is, whenever I speak to him, he looks like he's about to break down and cry. But when he's at his desk, when he thinks that no one else is looking at him, he spews confidence. That is the man I need to try to bring out. If I can give him the guts to bring that same confidence with him into every situation, he will exceed everyone's expectations of him.

Still, a part of me wanted to micromanage every little thing the kid did. Which included reading his reports over his shoulder at the same time he did. But I knew he would never find his own way if I did things that way. So, more often than not, I let him go through his papers first on his own before I decided it was time to look at them and see what was there. Chances are he got the same reports as I did while we were out in the field, though the detective in me didn't believe in coincidence. I knew I was going to have to have a look at them for myself at one time or another.

For thirty minutes, I kept an eye on him while he was reading. Looking for any little tell to see if there were any juicy nuggets left on his desk, while ignoring every word that I was reading from my own reports. So much so that I skimmed over the same paper three times before the words finally were ingrained into my brain; TRAN-SCRIPT OF CAMPUS POLICE PHONE CALL.

"Diamond!" I said as I held up the paper. "Did you get a copy of this?"

"Which one is that one?"

"The transcript. Did you get it?"

He shuffled through his stack again. "No, I don't see that one."

"Well, get your ass over here, then!"

As he rushed over to my desk, I started reading.

Operator: "MPD, Howard University Division, how may I direct your call?"

Caller: "I'd like to report a crime. An assault. I just came from a house on 6th and W, and there were four girls lying on the floor. There was a lot of blood. Blood was everywhere. Oh god, there was so much blood. I don't think they're going to make it. Send help, hurry!"

Operator: "Let me direct your call to Sergeant Scheffler. One moment, please."

Scheffler: "This is Sergeant David Scheffler. Where exactly is the house?"

Caller: "On W, right where 6th dead ends, I don't know the address. Two-story house. The girls are in the upstairs unit."

Scheffler: "Who lives there? Is it the occupants of the house who are lying on the floor?"

Caller: "Two of them, yes. The house belongs to Ruby-Sue Daniels and Deja Moore. They are both lying in blood on the floor. And so are Becca Wainwright and Stella Peters. Oh god, please do something. There was just so much blood. I don't think they'll make it."

Scheffler: "We have paramedics on the way there now. But if there's as much blood as you stated, it might be too late. How did you find the girls?"

Caller: (heavy breathing from the caller).

Scheffler: "Hello? Sir? How is it that you came to find
the girls? Do you live at the residence too?"

Caller: (phone clicks, ending transmission).

I stared at that last line for a few moments, trying to wrap my head
around the words that I had just read. The caller cut off when asked for
any personal information. That sounded more than a bit suspicious to
me. *Who could the caller be?* I asked myself. *Why did they hang up so
abruptly?*

Looking around the room for an inspiration, anything at all that
could make my mind grasp why the caller would report the crime
but not stay on the line to offer any more help. My gaze focused on
the potted plastic fern that was sitting next to the water fountain in
the room's corner. Diamond was mumbling something incoherent
behind me. I blocked him out, steadying my gaze on the fake plant—of
all things—instead. But that's when it dawned on me.

There's only two reasons for someone to phone in to report a
crime and then hang-up; they're involved, or they're trying to hide
something. Now we have to figure out which one it was. One thing
is for sure, the caller knew the victims. And if that's the case, we need
to talk to this person as soon as possible.

"Those are the same four names that we got earlier today at the
admissions office," I said aloud, as I placed the report back on top of
the pile of papers on my desk. My mind was in overdrive now. I needed
to think. Best to give the puppy dog an errand so I could focus.

"Better bring this to McFweed. This should help us get the names and addresses for next of kin," I said as I picked the papers back up handed the report to Diamond.

As he started off for the lieutenant's desk, I called out, "I'm gonna get on the horn to Sergeant Scheffler, see if we can't get a sit down with him."

"Sounds good, boss," he replied without even turning his head back towards me.

I normally get on him for using words like "boss" or "sir," but I think it actually helps the kid. He's used to having someone to report to. Someone that he gets his orders from. It makes sense. On patrol, you're always answering to someone on the other end of the radio, or your training officer, or the desk sergeant on your shift. It takes some time to get the sense that your partner is your equal.

As the phone rang on the other end while I awaited the Sergeant's answer, I wondered if the caller was our mystery man or if he was just an innocent bystander like he made himself out to be. Now, though, I wonder why he had hung up so abruptly and if he may have played a hand in the girls' demise after all. Questions that would soon be answered. The truth always seems to come out in the end. It was just the getting there part that I always seemed to have a problem with.

EDGEWOOD

December 21st, 12:10 AM

By the time Boyd had finally gotten his nerves under control and headed back to the apartment he shared with Jimmy, it was after midnight.

He saw the light on in his friend's bedroom, but decided another few hours of separation would probably do their friendship some good. He still had no clue what spooked Jimmy so badly, or even what he was going on about with the talk of the girls being dead.

He dropped his friend off on that street corner to steal a baseball card, and that is what he expected to happen. His mind couldn't grasp the curveball that had been thrown his way.

Either Jimmy had taken the card, or he hadn't. Those were the only two outcomes for their mission. There was no room for any gray areas or unforeseen mishaps in his black and white way of thinking.

The talk of dead people forced his mind to shut down as his fight-or-flight mode shifted heavily towards flight. Boyd peeled out of his parking spot on the curb by the pay phone, leaving Jimmy staring at him with his mouth agape as he drove away. He too had never felt more alone than he did at that moment. He knew he wasn't bright and that he leaned on Jimmy to make most of his decisions for him. But he also knew that something wasn't right by the way Jimmy was acting.

Three hours of driving aimlessly finally calmed him down enough to return home and face the consequences of leaving his friend all alone at the pay phone. Finally giving him enough nerve to take the chiding that he knew would inevitably come. To his surprise, what he heard coming from Jimmy's bedroom didn't have the sound of an irate parent, but more of a whimpering child.

After going to his own bedroom, Boyd swallowed hard and found yet another level of strength that he didn't know he even had. He returned to the slightly open door of his roommate and had a look inside. As he peeked in through the small crack in the door, the sounds from a few moments before became clearer as he watched his friend with his head in his fists on the edge of his bed, sobbing like a child.

"Hey, Jimmy," he said tentatively, "sorry for leaving you back there on the street corner."

"It's okay, Boyd. I know I scared you," Jimmy said as he looked at his friend with tear-soaked eyes. "Something bad has happened. Ruby-Sue is dead. I can feel it. There's no way she could survive with all of the blood there was."

"Did you get the card?"

"No, Boyd," he said in a defeated tone. "You're not understanding me. They're all dead. Ruby-Sue, Becca, Stella and Deja. They were all lying on the floor in the living room. Blood was everywhere. None of them were moving or making any noise." The tears started again.

"I freaked out and ran back to the car. I don't know who did this or why, but I couldn't be in there any longer than that. I ran. I didn't even try to help. Oh, God. It's all my fault," he cried out as his fists started pummeling the mattress he was sitting on.

Jimmy coughed up a wad of mucus as he tried to stifle the next fit of tears after his violent outburst. Boyd watched it come to land on his friend's bedroom carpet, not knowing what to say or do to comfort him. A sharp intake of breath let him know his friend was trying his hardest to stop his sobbing. The tears were flowing harder now though than when he had first entered the room.

Boyd, feeling uncomfortable and unsure of what to do next, slowly turned and headed back out the door as Jimmy said, "wait."

He stopped, turned back around to face his friend, but no more words came. Just the sounds of a man who seemed to be uncontrollably heartbroken.

Boyd turned to leave the room again, but this time, Jimmy reached his arm out to stop him. Jimmy stood, and while he normally towered over his friend, this time his body was too limp to reach its full height as he weakly collapsed into Boyd's body in a fearful but heartfelt embrace. His tears wetting the shirt at Boyd's shoulders.

"I don't know what to do," Jimmy's muffled voice said as his face was buried in the chest of his friend.

Taken aback by the reversal of the roles he now found himself in, Boyd gently pushed his friend away, taking a full step backwards so he could reassess the situation. He was no leader. He had no clue what to even say to comfort his friend. The next words out of his mouth surprised him.

"Grab your coat, Jimmy. I'm taking you to the police."

Jimmy grabbed his coat from the mess of dirty clothes on his bed and followed his friend to the front door mindlessly. Just like the phone call he made earlier in the evening, he knew that this was the right thing to do.

MPD MID-TOWN PRECINCT

December 21st, 5:01 PM

"**S**ergeant Scheffler, here. Who am I speaking with?"

"Yeah, Sarge, this is Max Denver with MPD Homicide. I just received a copy of the transcript from the call your guys received last night regarding the murders on campus. Was wondering when would be a good time to come over and pay you's guys a visit."

The Metropolitan Police Department staffed the Howard University Police. Though most of the coppers stationed over there were either rookies or cops waiting out their remaining days until their pensions came up. I haven't dealt with anyone from that office in an official capacity, but I knew a few men who had been shipped over there before.

We called it 'being sent out to pasture' around the precinct. Though it was a fine place for rookies straight out of the academy to cut their teeth in, it was the equivalent of getting the axe for the old timers.

From his voice, I couldn't get a read on the age of Sergeant Scheffler. But you don't make the rank of sergeant on a whim, so he must have a reputable past in the department. Must've been from one of the other precincts, though. No way I wouldn't have run into him at one point or another if he were stationed in our Mid-Town precinct.

"We're conducting follow-up interviews as we speak, so today might not be a good day for any meetings. I will keep you in the loop going forward," the Sergeant replied. "If you don't hear back from me by this time tomorrow, feel free to give me a call back. My personal desk number is (202) 555-7477."

"Sounds good," I said while lying through my teeth, hoping my animosity didn't convey through my voice. I was beyond miffed that he was holding out on me. This was my case, not his. University cops don't run homicide investigations. Never have and probably never will. Their only purpose in life is disciplining drunken college students. *Why was this guy getting in my way?*

I played nice anyway, knowing that if he had our guy in custody, playing his game was the only way I'd be able to get a run at him.

"Oh, and one more thing while I've got you on the line," I continued. "Did you happen to get the name of the caller?"

"No. He hung up before we could find out any information from him at all besides the location of the house. In a random turn of good fortune, though, he walked into our station a few hours after the phone call. His roommate brought him in. One of our officers is taking his statement now. We let him stew in the box for most of the day—making him sweat a little—checking in on him every hour or so. We wanted him to rethink the way he handled things last night. I was about to join in on things when your call came through. I will have one of my guys send over all the contact information once we conclude our interview with the two men. If we decide not to charge him, that is. You ask me, the kid looks guilty as sin."

"Is that right?" I asked suspiciously. This small-time copper wants to rule the narrative and take all the glory, it seems.

"Kid hasn't stopped crying for more than a minute since he's been here. Hasn't even dozed off for more than five."

I paused, taking in that last statement before proceeding. My anger was definitely on the rise, but I needed to keep my composure. No sense ruffling feathers right now. All that would do is make our job that much harder.

"In my experience, the ones that sleep are the ones who are guilty," I said in a passive-aggressive tone after my pause. Hoping that he would pick up on the fact that I was none too happy with getting the runaround here. "Ease passes through their entire body like a giant weight has been lifted off of their soul, thankful that they don't have to keep up their web of lies anymore."

"That could be, but this kid is involved, I can feel it," Scheffler said in a way that I knew was better not to be pressed. I still had to play his game if I wanted a chance at the kid. "I'm gonna get in there and see if I can't rub some sense into him and get a confession. I'll get everything over to you as soon as I can."

"Thanks, Sarge. Talk to you soon," I said before I returned the phone to its cradle on my desk. If my mind was in overdrive before, I had no idea what to call the speed it was turning at now. Waiting was one thing, but not being able to join in on a questioning was something of a whole different breed for me. Especially when I know the questioner is gunning for an admission of guilt. Add a little bit of anger to the mix, and you have a giant Max Denver powder keg waiting to explode.

I've worn down the carpets in the hallway outside of the interrogation room in our precinct from all the pacing I've done when I've not been allowed to join in on a questioning session. But at least when that happens, I'm in the same building and can get the knowledge I'm after as soon as the door opens. Or at least get to bear witness to the conversation through the false mirror of the interrogation room.

On this one, I may not know anything until a whole day from now. And if the Sarge thinks he's guilty before even sitting down with him, then that doesn't bode well for me and Diamond when our turn comes around to questioning him. People tend to clam up once the cuffs come out. Especially if they're not given the chance to tell their side of the story properly.

I've witnessed more than one interrogation when there was a preconceived notion that the perp was guilty, and I'll just say it's never pretty when that happens.

Doesn't matter what they say, or how they say it, the person asking the questions is only after one thing: a confession. And all that does is weaken the respect of all law enforcement in that perp's eyes, resulting in less communication that we actually need to do our jobs correctly. To say it's counterproductive would be an understatement.

But that is the way our legal system seems to be heading these days. Especially when dealing with people of color. God help us all if we plan on ever giving people an equal footing in this country. The damage has already been done for most.

Only good thing to come out of my conversation with Scheffler was the fact that if they did arrest this guy, we'd know exactly where to go to find him.

That thought wasn't sitting well in my stomach. With nobody in sight, I reached for my flask and took a swig of the hard stuff I kept close for instances such as these. Trying my hardest to put a lid on the boiling pot that was my anger. One won't hurt me. That's what I keep telling myself, at least. But with how many I've already had over the past couple of days, hopefully it would be my last one of the day.

As I was losing myself in the familiar and welcomed burn satisfying my senses, Diamond rounded the corner with what looked like a report of some kind in his hands. Quickly putting my flask back in its proper spot in the depths of my inside jacket pocket, I asked, "whatcha got there, Colio?"

"Fingerprint analysis from the crime scene."

"Let's have a look," I said while scooting my chair over to make some room for him, hoping I didn't reek of alcohol.

There were six usable sets of prints from the locations they dusted; the kitchen, the knife, the bottles of wine and wine glasses, the front doorknob—both inside and out—the picture frame that was broken in the bedroom and the window ledge.

Two sets were prominent throughout the home, with the exception of one place. The window ledge. And that specific print was only found on the ledge, the knife, and on the picture frame.

Bingo. We have a winner.

Now we had to hope that there would be a match somewhere in our database. No telling how long that would take. At least we now have something to take with us when we go back to Howard University to test against the two subjects they currently were holding.

Feeling a bit more optimistic than I was a few minutes ago—and with the added courage that was coming from my stomach—I felt that this was as good a time as any to knock off for the day. Nothing else either of us could do besides sit at our desks and wait for a phone call that may or may not come. So, I suggested to Cole, "why don't we go home for the night, get some sleep, and tackle these prints in the morning."

"Sounds good to me, boss," Diamond said as he was turning for the door before I could even lecture him about calling me 'boss' or fill him in on the conversation I had had with Sergeant Scheffler. Oh well, he'll have a pleasant surprise in the morning.

Grabbing my jacket, I started to plan my evening. A nice dinner with Sarah sounded like a wonderful idea. Something we haven't been able to do for a while now. Hopefully she won't mind coming to my place if I do the cooking.

THе Meтrо

December 21st, 7:57 PM

I stopped by a bodega on my way to the train station to pick some things up for dinner, namely a bottle of wine for Sarah and a few cans of soda for me.

Before heading out, I called Sarah's desk at her office to let her know I was leaving early and for her to grab what she wanted for dinner on her way over to my place. "Surprise me," I said. "I'll cook it if you buy it."

By early, I mean 8:00, not the usual midnight that I normally am leaving the station at. Her delight was well received through the phone.

Our date nights lately had been reduced to whenever my days off were, and that was only if she wasn't called in to work. Yes, she got called in to work in the middle of the night sometimes, too.

To say that dating in this profession was troublesome would be putting it nicely.

That's not to say we don't have our fair share of sleepovers, but even those have become less frequent as the lack of sleep starts taking its toll about an hour after I roll into the station. And catching killers is best done when fully alert. So, it has reduced us to seeing each other on a once per week schedule. Not ideal, but it beats the alternative.

We knew we had to enjoy our time together when we got it, especially if it was out of the blue. Like tonight seemed to be. So, I will make her some dinner while she enjoys a glass or two of wine. No booze for me, but the tradeoff is getting to have some real company in the house. A trade I would make seven days to Sunday if given the chance.

I'm not the culinary expert that my mother was, but I know my way around a kitchen. Or at least I did, before the wife moved out, that is. It is a nice feeling to create a home-cooked meal that is filled with love for a change. I had been so used to treating myself to peanut butter and jelly sandwiches—or whatever other pre-made meal that I picked up on the way home—that I forgot how nice it was to enjoy a meal at the dinner table with another person. Made me even forget that I wanted a drink most of the time. Man, what a difference a few months make, right?

With a grocery bag in one hand and my briefcase in the other, I strolled to the train station in anticipation of a night at home with Sarah. Well, I did wonder what Sarah was bringing over for me to cook, but other than that, my mind was free of anything case related.

That was the nice thing about having Sarah in my life. I was able to turn off my mind now. For the most part, at least. If we were close on a case, I'd still be up tossing and turning throughout the entirety of most of those nights. Other than that, once I left the doors of the station, my work-riddled brain stayed there.

As per usual, once in my seat on the train, my mind started going back to the case. I mostly used the train as a decompression unit. But if I'm being honest, it's usually the time for me to get low down and dirty with the conversations my gut had been trying to have with me throughout the day. This time was no different.

The six sets of fingerprints threw me for a loop all of a sudden. I thought nothing of it when we were going over the report, but now it stuck out like a giant red flag.

There were only five people in the apartment at the time of the murder. Or so we assumed. The four girls and the killer. Unless the killer had an accomplice. But that was something we hadn't even thought of. This had the look and feel of a revenge killing. The other three girls just fell victim to being in the wrong place at the wrong time. Nowhere in any of the reasoning or clues we had uncovered suggested there being more than one person involved in this brutal massacre.

But the one print that didn't seem to be anywhere else was found on the doorknob only. Both inside and out. Not at all where we assumed the killer had entered after we found the ladder in the alley. Which clearly shows our assumption was correct by there being only one set of prints on the window ledge. Hmm.

What is actually going on here? I asked myself.

Maybe this other person served as a of lookout of some sort. Or maybe gained entrance because he knew the girls, then made his way to the bedroom to unlock the window to allow the killer in. No, because then that set of prints would be on the sill too, and they didn't find them there. Only on the doorknob.

Maybe this other print belonged to a guest that left the get together early?

No, couldn't be that either. There were only four wine glasses set out. And there wasn't another one in the sink, or any other glasses for that matter, according to what Diamond had documented while doing his pass through the kitchen.

But there was the beer can that we grabbed. I'll have to remember to get a rush on prints for that evidence. That could be the deciding factor on if this was a team effort or not. Until then, I'm sticking with my gut. I still think this was a one-man job. Those other prints must have been from before.

So where does that leave us?

Frankly, I was at a loss. I was baffled. A sixth set of prints throws any theories I've had straight out the window. It made no sense at all to me.

I found myself getting flustered. All this was doing was getting my mind on a path where I didn't want it to go. I was looking forward to a nice dinner with my best girl, and now this extra set of fingerprints was invading my safe space. I have got to get this out of my mind until tomorrow, somehow. But I know that's a lost cause. Once I'm locked in on something, it takes an awful lot to dissuade me.

Sometimes, this job is completely unfair.

It's glorifying to put people in their place and get them off of the streets where they could do more harm, sure. But it was also guilty of stealing away all of your happiness without a moment's notice.

I tried my best to put it out of my mind, but I couldn't. It was definitely at the forefront now.

I was tempted to call Sarah and postpone dinner, but that wouldn't be fair to her.

I took my trusty notepad out of my briefcase and jotted down what was weighing on my mind. At least if I put my grievances in words, they would escape my mind for the time being. I also made a note to give Jack a call at some point during the day tomorrow to find out if he's been able to find anything on his end.

By the time I was finished writing my notes, the train was crossing over the river, signaling that my stop was coming up soon. I had spent most of the forty minutes completely lost in thoughts of the extra set of fingerprints.

As I bent down to put my notepad away in my briefcase, my flask just so happened to fall out at the same time. Quickly picking it up after the noise it made, I unscrewed the cap like it was second nature. I lifted it up to my mouth to take a drink, but the smell of the strong stuff made me stop before I went through with it.

Taking a deep breath—not because of the fumes, but more because my conscious decided now was a good time to intervene—I screwed the cap back on a put it away. Not back in my jacket pocket either, but in the paper bag that held our drinks for dinner. This way Sarah would see it and I could convince her to just take it from me once and for all. Can't take a drink without a cup. That sort of thing. But we will see how that plays out when we get there. Then again, maybe if I showed up smelling of hooch I would get better results. But I don't want a repeat of what happened on our first date.

The train slowed its pace as it neared my stop. Perfect timing, I thought. I was in one hell of a hurry to get home and get my mind off of the case all of a sudden. I gathered my belongings and disembarked my trusty iron horse as I headed off in the direction of my house.

Now back on flat ground, the anticipation of dinner started to become real again. I think maybe it's just that damn train that keeps my mind in work mode.

For too many years, that was my go-to place to get lost in my thoughts. No wife, no Jack, no phones ringing off the hook every fifteen seconds, no nothing. Just idle chatter from the other riders. But that was easy enough to get past.

One glance out the window—especially in the springtime as the cherry blossoms bloomed—and my mind could get lost in the beauty that this part of the country provides. Blocking out any sounds I did not want corrupting my thoughts.

Maybe that's why I'm so hard-headed about getting a vehicle of my own. As I witnessed earlier today, thinking and driving does not go well together for me. It may be a pain in the ass, but the purpose the train serves for me seems to help more often than hinder.

I pulled out my house key as I approached my front door. It's normally a quick ten-minute walk, but today I made record time. Must've been in a hurry to get out of the cold or something. The sounds of music playing from my RCA combo unit changed my perspective from a nearly dead silence I was walking in from, to one of great pleasure, knowing that Sarah was already there. The thought of us moving in together had been in my mind ever since our second first date—but I don't want to move too fast—so that thought has stayed tucked away in my brain for only me to fantasize about.

It's always nice to get home early, especially in the middle of a case. Knowing that we had a date night planned meant that my mind could really get some rest tonight, too. "Hi, honey, I'm home," I said, as I removed my jacket and hat. Placing them on the back of the couch that sits just behind the front door of my home.

Not hearing any reply, I walked into the kitchen. No sign of her there either, so I continued to the hallway towards the bedrooms. It was there that I saw her on my bed, a glass of wine in hand, wearing nothing else but a smile. Her finger curled and wagged in a "come here" motion. I dropped the bag I was holding and joined her.

"Dessert before dinner? I could get used to this," I said with a smile and a teasing laugh.

As I started to disrobe, I heard the noise of my worst nightmare coming from the kitchen.

Pulling my pants back on, I ran to the telephone to answer it before it stopped.

Wrong move.

I should have just let it ring.

ARLINGTON, VA
December 21st, 9:29 PM

"We got a confession!" Cole shouted over the phone. He must've stayed behind at his desk finishing paperwork instead of heading home when I did. Rookie mistake. He'll learn quickly that when you get the chance to knock off early, you take it without asking any questions.

"You're shittin' me, right?" I asked. Even though from my conversation with Scheffler earlier, I shouldn't have been surprised. He seemed hell bent on getting that confession no matter what.

"Nope, just got off the horn with Sergeant Scheffler. He was rather proud of the fact that he got the kid to sing," Cole explained. "He was ringing your desk, but since you weren't here, I answered. How come you didn't tell me there was a suspect in custody?"

"Slipped my mind, kid." A white lie. "Besides, you was bringing the names of the victims to McFweed when I spoke to him. I figured they had nothing rock solid to hold him on and that we'd get a chance to talk to him tomorrow after they cut him loose. I was waiting to hear back from Scheffler to get his contact information. Guess I was wrong. But grab those fingerprint cards and come pick me up. Let's get over to their holding cell before the kid gets sent to central booking."

"Roger that. Give me thirty."

Feeling both optimistic and dejected at the same time, I hung up the phone and returned to the bedroom.

"How much time do we have?" Sarah asked as I came back in. She had already started pulling her clothes back on. She knew the drill. Phone calls this late only amounted to one thing: work.

"About half an hour." My face must've conveyed my annoyance.

"Okay, well, I'll be right here waiting for you when you get back. We can make dinner for breakfast tomorrow morning or something instead," she offered, with some softness to her voice.

Smiling, and thankful that she was so understanding, I crept onto the bed next to her and laid down flat on my back. On the one hand, I was upset that our night had been ruined, but on the other, I knew that this could be the breakthrough that we had been looking for. I knew what had to be done. Dinner plans would have to wait. No matter how upsetting that was to either of us. Another perk of the job.

"Before you go, I want to tell you something that I found when I developed my photos this afternoon," she said, continuing with the gentleness in her voice, as if speaking in any other way would catapult me over the edge somehow.

"At first glance, I thought it was nothing," she continued. "But as I took out my loupe, I could see that there was some sort of writing in the blood next to one of the bodies. Just like as if it were a child's finger painting. Three letters were written there in the blood, plain as day and unmistakable when magnified. The letters spelled out MRE. I can't make any sense of it, but it clearly was written there for a reason. There's no way her hand had made those markings on accident. Even if she was dragged, which clearly, she wasn't, a hand wouldn't make those letter groupings without a conscious effort."

"Hmm. That's interesting. Did you bring copies of the photographs over here with you tonight?"

"Yep. I was planning on showing them to you after we ate. I don't know if it means anything, but if you're going back out tonight, this information might end up helping in your investigation."

"It damn well might. Seems like our victim might be trying to tell us something. Maybe even identifying her killer. Diamond and I are heading back over to Howard tonight to question a perp that the University cops think is good for this. They booked him about an hour ago. Seems they got a confession out of him. I want the chance to question him before he gets shipped over to Central, check his prints against the ones we have, and find out what brought him forward after he initially ran."

"Sounds like you're gonna be out all night."

"Hopefully not, but you know how these things go. Can't sit and wait when we might have a run-on things. That's burned me too many times in the past."

We both fell silent as we embraced each other on top of the bed, subconsciously counting down the minutes until Diamond showed up.

SOMEWHERE IN MARYLAND

December 22nd, 12:59 AM

H e drove in silence.

The blurred white lines of Route 1 put his mind into a dream-like state as images of Ruby-Sue and the others lying in pools of their own blood corrupted his thoughts. Ruining whatever pleasant images he had once had of their time spent together as a couple forever. The bulge in his jacket pocket from his stolen prize reminded him that this was no dream at all. This was reality.

It was never supposed to end up the way it did. And not just the murders, either, but the entire relationship that the two of them had shared. They happened to get close to one another by chance. Fate, as he liked to call it. Though the attraction was immediate, he thought she was out of his league. Yet they somehow found their way to each other, anyway.

He knew he was playing with fire even contemplating such a relationship. But the war had ruined him, and he needed to find solace in anything he could. The army turned him into a killing machine—taking the damaged teenager that he was when his number was called and building him up to be the soldier that they desired. Which ultimately was something that he hated about himself as he tried to readjust to civilian life once he came back home. Ruby-Sue helped with that, but he knew it was only a matter of time until those urges resurfaced. He just never thought that she would be the one to give those same urges the rise that they got.

His first kill gave him nightmares. Sleepless for several days because he couldn't erase the memory of that dead Nazi's eyes as the life escaped from his body. Every time he lay his head down at night, that piercing gaze sent his stomach into convulsive knots. He begged for forgiveness from the Lord above, shameful for his number being called in the draft that sent him over there in the first place. Turning him into the monster that he was today. But the past is the past. And that was something that he couldn't change no matter how hard he tried.

Yet, despite his hatred for what he had become, he killed again. And again, after that, too. He killed so many times that it became second nature for him. And now he had done it again once more. But this time, the consequences were far higher. Now he would never have the chance to win back the love of his life. Ruby-Sue was gone, and so was his shot at living the normal life that he so craved.

All because that punk kid came between them. That's who he should've focused his anger on. But when he saw red, something else took over. It had been that way since he was a child, though now he knew how to corral that anger. How to maximize it to do the most damage possible. Oh, that punk kid will most definitely get his, he thought. Might not be today. Or even tomorrow. But when this is all said and done, Jimmy Malone will still be in his sights. And assignments never get forgotten.

Arlington, VA

December 21st, 10:04 PM

The knock on the door startled us both. I gave Sarah a kiss on her cheek as I got up and gathered my things. She had fallen asleep. I could tell by her look of confusion when I shot up off of the bed at the sound coming from the front door. As I caught a glimpse of the clock on top of my nightstand, I saw it was already after ten. It was going to be a long night indeed.

Diamond was already back in the car by the time I finally made it outside. I stopped in the bathroom to splash some water on my face before heading out. I didn't mean to, but I had fallen asleep too and had to do something to shake away the grogginess that I was feeling. I needed to be fully alert for this questioning session.

"I know you said earlier that I need to be more assertive and stand my ground," Cole said once I had joined him on the bench seat next to him in our car, "but I would be lying if I said I didn't feel like you left me out of the loop with this suspect."

"You know, Cole, you're absolutely right. But I was testing you again. To see if any of our conversation from earlier today had actually stuck," it was a complete lie, but the kid had me dead to rights and I wasn't about to admit that to him yet.

"I wanted to see how you would handle information being withheld from you," I continued. "As detectives, this sort of thing happens on a daily basis. We get the runaround from witnesses, we get the runaround from other jurisdictions. Hell, we even get the runaround from our own partners from time to time. I wanted to see how you handled yourself when something like this arose. It's not like I was going to catch three trains to run all the way over to Howard to question this suspect without you. You see how silly that sounds now?"

"Yeah, I guess you're right, Max," he said with the same moodiness from this morning. "I just felt that we had a breakthrough and were finally on even footing, is all. That's why it hurt to find out about this suspect from someone else."

"First off, we're not even close to being on even footing. Secondly, every scenario we face is a learning experience. For me too, not just for you. And C, I'll repeat what I said to you earlier today; grow a pair and get over it." I could feel my voice rising as the effects of my dozing off were apparently taking over. All of a sudden, I was in no mood to deal with his crybaby bullshit. "You're a detective in the most important city in the world. That's something to take pride in. Start showing it. Stop moping when something doesn't go your way and be a man. Take action and put the ball back in your court. Okay, lesson over."

I could tell it rattled him. I honestly don't even have a good explanation for why I didn't tell him. I just kept it to myself for selfish reasons. The same selfish reasons that I was trying to get rid of along with my drinking. The two go hand in hand. And now that I think about it, when all of that happened was about the same time I took a swig off of my flask.

Regardless, *I* have to do better if *he* is ever going to do better. I think I swung it in a way that was believable to him. That I was using it as a learning tool. At least I hoped I did. Only time will tell if it worked or not. I shook my head and got my mind back on the task at hand. Something still wasn't adding up to me.

We sat in silence for the rest of the drive. It took us about thirty minutes to get across the state line and all the way to the other side of the city. By the time we pulled up to the small, one room precinct that was the Howard University sub-station, I think he had finally cooled down.

I led the way in, but I handed Cole my notebook to add to the papers he was carrying. "Take the lead on this, son. Show me what you're made of."

I held the door open for him as I watched him march up to the officer manning the desk. "Sergeant Scheffler, please. I am Detective Cole Diamond, and this is my partner, Detective Max Denver."

"One moment," the officer said, holding a single finger up to let us know he would be right back. "Let me see if he's still here."

The officer went around the corner to a room with a closed door and a nameplate that was too small to read from where I was standing. The room was small—probably about the size of a bedroom in an apartment—and made it hard for me to believe there was any room for a whole separate room in the layout plans. Besides the desk that the officer was behind when we walked in, the rest of the room was empty save for a few Howard posters on the wall and a wastebasket next to the desk.

I got the feeling that this was probably the biggest case these university cops had ever been involved in, though they didn't show it.

Small precinct or not, they were still a part of the Metropolitan Police Department. And we only allow first class cadets to make it through the graduation process. Still, it emitted the feeling that Diamond and I were a couple of big city detectives trying to bully our way into a small town crime. Maybe that was where the animosity that I felt from Sergeant Scheffler earlier was coming from.

The officer from the desk returned with a short, but stocky, blond-haired man with a face you'd like to punch, in tow. I could tell by the stripes on his sleeve that he was the man in charge around here.

"Sergeant Scheffler," the short man said with his hand held straight out, awaiting shakes from the two newcomers in his precinct. I shook first, then deferred to Diamond to take the lead.

"I'm Diamond, this is Denver," Cole said as he shook hands with the Sergeant.

Diamond towered over him by a good six inches but didn't give the aura of being a man who was trying to take charge. That's something else I'll have to work with him on, though while we're guests in another man's precinct, it's probably best that he didn't take the alpha approach that I often do. Respect is warranted within the company of sergeants' stripes.

Diamond fumbled his words and muffed his opening line—which was to be expected—allowing all the control to go right back to the sergeant.

Taking charge, especially mentally, is the only way to assert yourself as the alpha in the room. And sometimes that is the difference between getting all the information you've come for, or leaving empty-handed after letting yourself get the runaround. Luckily, I was there too, and I stepped up to the plate and took over.

Hey, I gave the kid his chance. He'll get it. Maybe not today, but he'll get it. Like I've said before, patience isn't my strong suit. Especially at damn near eleven o'clock at night after my evening with Sarah had been ruined. Respect for the sergeant or not, I wasn't going to let the kid get trampled over.

"Yeah, Sarge," I said with some authority as I stepped out from behind Cole, "we spoke on the telephone earlier today. My partner has some fingerprint cards of the prints we lifted from the crime scene that we'd like to match up with your suspect. And, time allowing, we have a few questions for him as well."

"Sure thing," Scheffler said. "Follow me and we can go over the prints before I take you in to see him. Luckily it's Christmas break. We only have the one cell here on campus, so you should be able to talk freely in there. He's our only prisoner at this time. I know this is your case, and I hope you don't think we were stepping on your toes by placing him under arrest, but he confessed to being in the house. Seemed like it was open and shut to me."

"Well, that's why we're here. We've got nothing on our end, yet. Just some prints to look at. But we've got a damn good idea of whose prints were left where, which was why we brought the print card with us. Did he offer anything else up other than being in the house?"

"Not really. Something about some baseball card, but that's about it. If you'll allow it, I'm gonna hold everything else close to the vest until after you guys have your chat with him. I wanna see if he says the same thing to you as he did to us."

"That's not really protocol," I growled, wondering who this guy thought he was. "If you was trying to hide anything to get the glory of this collar yourself, you probably wouldn't have said anything about it. So I'll allow that as a courtesy. One copper to another, and all."

I was still a little perturbed by our conversation from earlier today, and I wanted him to know that. This may be his first actual case in years, but that didn't mean he could sit back and withhold information. That's not how things work in the Metropolitan Police Department. And I was going to make sure he damn well remembered that.

"Thanks," he said begrudgingly. "We're still not done transcribing the interview yet, so by the time you're done with him, it should be complete and then we can go over it all together before you head out."

I nodded in agreement and fell in behind the Sergeant as we left through a back door that led us momentarily outside before we entered an adjacent building behind the one we had just left. The cold air doing its best to cool off my hot temper.

Seemed to me that their precinct consisted of a few smaller modular units that encompassed their entire station. Quite a difference from our precinct. Once we ran out of room on the first floor, they started moving different departments upstairs to different stories. Now each floor housed its own unit of the MPD. I've got no clue what other businesses or office spaces were evicted to make room for my brothers of the badge. That had all happened before I took the oath.

"Welcome to the crime lab," Scheffler said with a smirk as he pointed to a single desk that stood next to a surveyor's desk. There were several black smudge marks all over the white surface, telling me they had done their fair share of fingerprinting in this tiny office. Probably a lot of rowdy frat parties behind the ghosts of those prints. This is a college campus, after all.

As he said earlier, it was Christmas break, and there appeared to be only one set of prints that had been worked on recently. I gave Diamond a nod, and he pulled out the print cards as he grabbed the stool to have a seat at the desk.

He looked up at me in a panic the second he sat down. I quickly realized what had gotten him into a tizzy.

"Do you happen to have a loupe my partner can use? We've been having problems keeping an eye on ours back home, so company policy is it is not to be removed from the premises," I asked Scheffler. Diamond gave me a look of thanks before turning his reddened face back to the cards on the desk.

"Absolutely. I know exactly what you're talking about. Bottom left drawer. If you reach underneath, you'll feel the handle."

With Cole now fully equipped, we left him to go over the prints. Though he's not formally trained to analyze prints, every hopeful that goes through the academy has been given the basic gist of what to look for when comparing fingerprints: whirls, loops and ridges. The defining characteristics that make each fingerprint unique.

Scheffler and I bumped gums about this and that and nothing all together while we waited for Diamond to check over the cards. The tension from a few moments prior seemed to be gone for the time being.

Even though I'm not one for socializing, whenever I run into another badge, it seems the words come out of my mouth with ease. Maybe because I know exactly what the other has been through to get to where they are in their career.

We gabbed for about fifteen minutes before Diamond looked over to us and said: "Jimmy Malone."

Scheffler looked like he had a smile on the verge of making itself known. "That's the name the kid gave us."

Diamond looked up from the desk and gave me a half smile after Scheffler let us know we were on the right path. I gave him a nod, letting him know non verbally that he had done a good job.

"Okay, Sarge," I said, interrupting Cole's victory lap, "now that we know who we're dealing with, let's say you let us have a shot at him."

"So, do his prints fit the narrative you two think you have?"

"The suspect told you he was in the house, and the prints confirm that."

Pettiness has always been a flaw of mine, and I continued with it here. If Scheffler wanted to withhold his own information, I planned to do so, too. "Now, if you'll be so kind to show us the way there, we can sort this out."

Scheffler didn't seem to like the fact that he wasn't privy to the information in my head. Despite this, he led us to an adjacent building housing only one cell. He quickly took his leave, presumably to have a look in on us from a closed circuit feed in one of the other buildings.

"Mister Malone," I said as Diamond and I pulled up a couple of chairs. "I'm Max Denver with the Metropolitan Police Department. This is Detective Cole Diamond. We have a couple of questions for you."

COLUMBIA HEIGHTS
December 21st, 12:57 AM

B oyd was on the verge of tears as he was led into the interrogation room across the hall from the one they took Jimmy into.

He had never stepped foot into a police station before in his life, let alone an interrogation room. The coldness of the room—with its metal furniture and flat-gray painted walls—left Boyd questioning whether bringing Jimmy in was the right call or not. If he had known that he was going to be questioned as a witness, he would have left Jimmy to cry in his room by himself back at home.

The minutes ticked by slowly as they left him with only the thoughts in his head to keep him company. A police officer had shown him in, told him where to take a seat, and then left back out the door again. Boyd was almost too confused with what was happening to focus on what he would say when another officer finally came in to question him. If they ever came back, that is.

His fragile mind couldn't comprehend what was going on. Why was he the one in the room when it was Jimmy who might have been the one to do harm to Ruby-Sue and her friends? Questions like that one bounced around in his head while he wondered if this was what jail was like.

Boyd had seen a picture or two in the cineplex about life on the inside. And whenever a prisoner was led into a room like the one he was in now, it never turned out good for the person being questioned. The cops always got their man in those movies, and he wondered how long it would be until he had handcuffs slapped on him, too. Was this his life now?

But he had done nothing wrong. He kept telling himself that over and over again, without understanding the fact that he was an accomplice to whatever it was that went on earlier. As the minutes turned to hours, with still no word on what was going to happen to him, he laid his head down on the table and slept.

HOWARD UNIVERSITY SUB-STATION HOLDING CELL

December 21st, 10:56 PM

The kid looked young. Too young to be sitting in a jail cell on multiple murder charges. But it was his decisions that led him here, not mine, so I can't feel sorry for him.

He was lounging with his back propped up against the wall of his jailhouse bed when we walked in. He gave the appearance of feeling at home behind the bars of his cell—not giving a single thought to the severity of the claims against him. His short afro was flattened in the back by hours of resting his head against the hardness of the wall.

He didn't look up to meet our eyes as we approached him. But he didn't cower or try to hide his sight line, either. Giving me the impression that he was trying to keep up the facade of being a hardened criminal. Too bad the redness of his eyes gave away his secret that he has spent a lot of hours passing time spilling tears since he had been in there.

He couldn't be any older than twenty-two years old, I thought. Though his face showed lines of stress that made him look a lot older than he actually was. Probably because of a life of crime or whatever other reasons he felt that he needed to be in a hurry to grow up instead of taking it slow. Like so many other men his age had done.

The kid looked tired, too. The bags under his eyes were swollen to the point to where if you touched them wrong, they looked like they would explode with liquid.

"Can you state your name for the record, please?" I asked him, knowing full well that we didn't have any sort of voice recorder with us. Not knowing if they set the jail cell up for audio recording or not, I wanted to go by the book. It was better to be safe than sorry. There's nothing worse than getting a confession—or any other substantial piece of evidence—thrown out by a judge because you didn't follow protocol.

"Jimmy Aaron Malone," the kid said, still not giving us the benefit of looking directly at us.

"So, let me get this straight, Mr. Malone. According to the telephone transcript from when you reported the crime, you were the one who found the bodies. Is that correct?" I asked, easing into the questioning with a softball question. One that was easy to answer. And one that we already knew the answer to.

"Yes," he replied coldly.

He wasn't interested in playing our game; it seemed. One-word answers were nothing new to me. It was a way for the interviewee to control the conversation. Or so they thought. This kid looked like he had been in an interrogation room or two before in his day, so it would definitely take some guile on our part to get him to talk. Still, he was just a kid. I've dealt with scumbags ten times worse than this.

I'll break him, I thought. *In probably less than ten minutes*, I wagered to myself.

"What brought you to the residence on that night?" I continued.

"To be honest," he said as he perked up on his cot, putting his feet on the ground and facing us for the first time, "I was going to break in. But when I heard music coming from the inside, I decided to try the front door instead of trying to pick the lock."

Ding ding ding. That answer was setting off fire alarms within my body.

"What made you think it was okay to let yourself in?" I asked. Most people would become spooked if the house they were planning on robbing seemed to have occupants inside. "Don't seem like the smartest thing to do. You stupid or somethin', kid? That why you just barged in uninvited?"

Rapid-fire questions back to back to back usually start a perp reeling while their lies start to pile up. Usually we would have the benefit of the doubt in knowing most of the information in the questions we ask, but not this time. We were going into this interview blind. I hoped that we would be able to pick up on any abnormalities on the fly.

"No, no, no," he pleaded while backpedaling.

"You have it all wrong. I didn't hurt those girls. They were like that when I got there!" Tears once again welled up in his hardened eyes.

"So who killed them, then? Seems pretty convenient that you went there to rob the house and its inhabitants were dead on arrival. Did you have an accomplice? Were you the distraction so they could come in through the window and kill the girls so it would be easier to rob them?" I asked, continuing with multiple questions at once and getting to the hard points earlier than I usually would. Mainly because

I wanted to see his reaction to the use of the window as an entrance, but partly because of the wager I had made with myself too. Who were we kidding?

Besides, I doubted Scheffler had even brought that up, or if he even knew about the window. Hard to say what information got passed down to him by the uniforms at the scene. Probably just slapped the cuffs on the kid as soon as he said he was at the house.

"I ain't got no idea who killed them! They were already on the floor when I got there. There was just so much blood everywhere! It's like a nightmare every time I close my eyes now. I don't think I'll ever be able to unsee what I saw that night." Tears were now flowing with ease as his temper seemed to come to a boil.

His face weakened. That outburst seemed to take a blow to his tough-guy composure. Staring at the wall behind my head, then back directly at my face before going back to the wall behind my left ear, he became silent. It was a pause I was grateful for. It's moments like these when I can really get a read on who I'm up against. And if I'm being honest, I don't think this kid has the guts to be a killer. Not in a million years.

I've seen murderers cry before, but that was because their game was up. They got caught, and their fantasies could no longer be played out in real life. But this? This was different. This kid was scared. Bona fide scared.

"Boyd was with me, but he stayed back in the car. He didn't even come to the house with me. He was just my driver," he continued after a few long and deep breaths to get his composure back in order.

"Who is Boyd?" Diamond asked, jumping straight back into the thick of things after the long pause a moment ago. I gave him a look, letting him know that that was the right question at the right time.

"Boyd Perkins. He is my friend and roommate. I look after him. He's a little slow. He had nothing to do with this, I swear," he said in short, controlled answers with a stone-cold sobering look. Seemed pretty clear he was adamant about this Boyd character not having anything to do with any of this.

"It was my idea to rob Ruby-Sue," he continued. "Nobody was supposed to be there. Ruby-Sue said she was leaving that morning to go back home to Philadelphia for Christmas. The snow storm must have kept her here though. So that's why I asked him to drive me, because the house was supposed to be empty. He was never a part of the plan. He was only there to drive me, I swear. Leave him out of this."

"It's a little late for that, Mr. Malone. Boyd is already a part of this. As of right now, we have enough to arrest him as an accomplice to robbery, at the very least. Maybe even co-conspirator to murder, depending on how the rest of these questions go," I added, digging deeper into the layers of the story. I wanted to see how loyal Mr. Malone would be to his friend once the heat got turned up a bit on him.

"No!" He shouted, showing us the first signs of passion since we walked into the cell house. "Leave Boyd out of this. He didn't even step foot onto the property. He let me out a few blocks away on Oakdale. He stayed there the whole time. Then he drove me to a pay phone on Rhode Island Ave. That's where I made the call to the cops. He didn't even wait for me. He went back home because it scared him when I came back out to the car."

"Why would he be scared? Did you tell him you killed the girls?" I asked.

"No!" He shouted again. "I already told you I didn't kill them. He was scared because I told him they were all dead."

"Why the change of heart?" Diamond asked, trying to figure out why he would call in the crime if he was the one that killed them. "Why make that phone call?"

I nodded at him again, letting him know I echoed his thoughts on the phone call.

"Because someone has to pay for this!" He shouted a third time. "That was my girl that I saw there on the floor. I didn't know if there was still time to save her or not. I knew I couldn't save her, and it would look ten times worse if I had her blood on me when the cops showed up, so I ran. I had Boyd take me to a pay phone far enough away from the house that we wouldn't look like suspects."

"Oh, so you did know the girls then?" I asked, giving pause afterward to let the question sink in. Sometimes the best way to get a perp to talk is to remain silent. The absence of noise fills their mind with guilt and they spew information that they normally would keep to themselves. Almost like a guilt identifying defense mechanism.

After a few moments of silence, he finally spoke again.

"Yes, I knew them. I knew all of them. Ruby-Sue was my girl. The other three were her friends. Becca, Stella and Deja. Ruby-Sue told me she was leaving for Philly yesterday morning, like I already told you," he said somberly. His face staring at the wall directly in front of him, his eyes fixed on a single spot, not wavering once while he spoke. The guilt of what he was saying aloud seemed to haunt his brain. "That's why I went there last night. I thought the coast would be clear. Like I said before. I didn't kill them. They were already dead when I got there."

"So you want us to believe that you went to the house to rob it—the house of your girlfriend, knowing that she wouldn't be home—yet we find four dead bodies there instead? Do you know how idiotically stupid that sounds? Do you think we're imbeciles, Mr. Malone?" I barked. Not an ounce of sympathy in my voice at all. It was the voice I usually used when I was done playing games and wanted the perp to know I was onto them.

"There's no point in trying to make you believe what I am telling you," he said with a steady voice. One that was in control of the situation for the moment. Surprising both Diamond and myself at the same time. It was a tone of voice that begged to be listened to. And heard. One that we had yet to hear out of the kid. One of a person a lot smarter and wiser than my partner and I had given him credit for.

"Either you believe me or you don't," he continued with his lecture. "Now, I've already told you I was in the house. In fact, I'm sure you already have my fingerprints to tell you that much, which is why you're here talking to me. But you keep talking about accomplices and windows and stuff. That tells me you know you don't have the right guy, or at least that you don't know the whole story. So why are you pressuring me? Why aren't you listening to what I'm telling you? If there were prints on the window, you already know they ain't mine. So why you still hassling me?

"You just see me as just another black kid, don't you? So I must be guilty, right? Is that it? I knew the girls and admitted to being in the house, so you're just gonna lock me up and throw away the key without even looking for anybody else. Am I right? Shit. I don't even know why you wasted your gas coming over here to talk to me. Y'all already have me pegged as guilty. And I'm sure the campus cops told you the same thing. I'm done talking to you. You two do what you have to do, but I'm done."

I mumbled something under my breath, but couldn't make the words come out. His outbreak silenced me to the point where I didn't even know where to take this next. I was both astonished and amazed at the points he was making. And I felt for him terribly. He was right. And I felt guilty just being associated with his train of thought.

He had made a good point, though. One that I had already been thinking of throughout this whole interview. His story added up. We only found his prints on the front door. Nowhere else in the house. Not on the window ledge, not on the knife. Nowhere else at all. Which brings me back to my questioning the reason why Scheffler even slapped cuffs on the kid in the first place when there was so much more evidence to go over.

Now, I do know that questioning the kid here was a lot easier than having to track him down somewhere else. Even so, something was still off about the whole thing. I wasn't ready to cut him loose and apologize to him. Not yet, anyway. Not when he could still be of help.

I had to find a way to press him on the ex-boyfriend somehow, but unfortunately I think we had lost our leverage. He was angry. His trust was gone. If he had any to begin with, that is. Maybe leaving him in there for another night would do him some good. But I didn't want to play it that way. There's a time for playing the bad cop role, and I didn't think that this was it. Not when his ego was being battered. But sometimes it's the only option worth playing.

"Yes, you're absolutely correct, Mr. Malone," I said, after taking some time to formulate a new plan of attack.

"We do have your prints. They were found at the crime scene. Hence the reason you are behind these bars right now," I said, while pointing to the cold steel barrier that was between us and the kid. "But I also know that you're holding out on me. And until you want to fess up to what you know, you'll continue to sit behind these bars. But just to let you know, the longer you hold out, the harder this becomes for you.

"Any moment now, a van will come and drag you down to central booking. It gets pretty crowded over there. It already looks like you've gotten zero sleep, and you can count on getting zero more once you're there. So, you wanna talk, or should we leave you to your stewing?" I continued, trying to press the situation that any help he gives us now will ultimately help him in the long run.

"You cops are all the same, aren't you? Young negro kid, at the house, must be the one who did it. But I'm telling you the truth!" He screamed. Anger once again was filling the void. His voice echoed off the walls of the mostly empty room. "There's no doubt about that. Why would I call the cops if I was the one who did it? Think about that for a moment, if you're capable of even doing that. There are always two sides to every story, Sir. The side that I'm telling you is the truth."

"No need to get testy, son," I said, trying to reel in his anger before it got too far out of hand. "We just want to know who killed these girls. That's all. You give us the name, and you're free to go."

Bargaining chip on the table. Now to see how he wants to play it.

"I don't know who did it. If I did, they'd be dead right now, too. And that's a promise," he gnashed his teeth with the force of a vise as he stared me down while he spewed his vow.

"Okay, let's back it up a bit, then. Why were you at the house that night?" Diamond asked, trying to be the voice of reason it seemed. "You went there to rob it, right? But what were you after?"

"Babe Ruth. That's what I was after."

Perplexed by that answer, Diamond and I exchanged questioning looks. The kid must have picked up on it and elaborated further.

"Ruby-Sue had a Babe Ruth baseball card in a picture frame in her bedroom. Her father had given it to her before he died. She didn't care about baseball, or really even know anything about it. Not the way Boyd and I did. She only knew that it was worth a little bit of money and that her dad had told her how special the card was. But that baseball card is worth thousands. I thought that if me and Boyd could get our hands on it, that things would really start to change for us."

"So, let me get this straight," I interjected. "You were going to rob your girlfriend of something that was obviously sentimental to her? And you're telling me you think we're the stupid ones?"

"I know how stupid that sounds right now, but me and Boyd just wanted a better life and we thought that if we had that card we could sell it and get some real money."

"So those tears were just an act? Is that right?" I asked.

"No! I loved her, I swear. She was my girl!"

"You loved her enough to rob her? Tell me how that makes sense. Tell me how you think a jury of your peers will convey that? You claim to love her, but you were only interested in what she had. So what makes you think they will believe you when you say you didn't kill them? Weren't the girls just in the way of what you thought you needed to have a better life?"

"Look," he said. "I know how this looks. Trust me. I've been kicking myself all day and night about even thinking of taking that card. But the fact of the matter is, if I didn't go to the house that night, we still wouldn't know that they were dead. They'd still be laying there waiting to be found. So, in a sense, I did your job for you. Am I proud of what my intentions were? No! But I can't go back on that now. I'm innocent and you know it!"

"So, where's the card now? Did you already sell it?" Diamond asked.

The question seemed to freeze the kid. Which gave my assumptions some merit. He didn't know the card was gone yet. I could tell in his face before he even muttered his next words.

"I... I don't know," he stuttered. "I didn't even make it into the bedroom. I left the house as soon as I saw their bodies on the floor. The sight of all of that blood spooked me something fierce. Babe Ruth was the last thing on my mind once I seen what I seen."

I knew he was telling me the truth. But I couldn't let him know that. It would ruin whatever leverage we still had. And right now, that was the only thing we had in this case. If he was innocent of the crimes of murder, we were back at square one.

"Then tell me this, then. Who else knew about the card? She obviously didn't keep it hidden. I saw the picture frame where it was kept. I even read the note from her father. Did any of your other friends know about it and beat you to the punch?"

"No. Boyd is the only other person I ever even mentioned it to. We weren't trying to share our wealth with everybody. We wanted it for us, and only us."

"What about the guy she was seeing before you? What's his name?" I asked, trying to finally get a bead on my new number one suspect.

"I don't know his name. She never told me. She always joked about him being this mysterious guy, even going so far as painting a question mark on her bedroom wall, but I've got no clue who he is." Which brought my mind back to the painting I had seen the day before while in her bedroom. It had definitely caught my attention, but I had given it little thought since. Who knew that it would become the clue we had been looking for this entire time.

"The only thing she ever even mentioned to me about him was that she had to keep him a secret because of his job," he continued, with a look of confusion in his eyes. "If his employers ever found out about their relationship, he'd be terminated on the spot. So, I left it alone. I figured he was out of her life and wouldn't be a problem since she was with me now."

I had to hand it to the kid. He seemed to handle himself with more composure than I would've thought. Not only did he find his girlfriend dead, but now also his ticket to a better life was missing too. Instead of cashing in on a big payday, he now was on the precipice of throwing his life away to the system. Once a colored kid gets the legal hooks in them, it was damn near impossible to break free of that. Despite that, the kid was talking and cooperating with us, knowing that the ending didn't look too favorable to him.

"And you don't know what this guy did for work? How about his age? Was he older than Ruby-Sue or were they around the same age?" Diamond asked, proving to me he definitely has been paying attention to what I've been teaching him. Each time he has chimed in tonight, it's been the right question at exactly the right time. I'll have to remember to give him credit for that later.

"Like I said before, I don't know anything about him. Not what he does for work, or his age, or where he lives. The guy is a ghost to me." His tears had long since subsided by this point in time, leaving only the redness of his sore and tired eyes as evidence that they ever existed.

Now it seemed that the kid was actually trying to do what was in the best interest of his dead girlfriend. I actually don't know how to break the news to him that I believe what he's been telling us, but that we can't let him free. Not tonight, anyway. He'll still be sent to central booking and processed for the four murder charges over there, most likely. The best I can offer him is that I'll plead my case with McFweed in the morning, and hopefully, that will be enough. Not much of a consolation prize for cooperating with us, but that's the breaks sometimes.

"Thank you for speaking with us, Mr. Malone. I know how hard reliving the past few days has been for you, but we appreciate all the help you have given us. Hopefully, we are one step closer to finding out who did this to your friends," I said with as much gratitude as I could give him without sounding phony.

"So that's it, then? Do I get to go home now?"

"Unfortunately, no, that's not exactly how it works. It's too late in the evening now to do anything about it, anyway. Since you were arrested for the murders, that means the DA thinks they have enough to take you to trial, so getting you out of this will take a bit of time. Especially since the arresting officer cites a confession as the reason you were arrested, whether we think that was legitimate or not. You'll probably still be brought down to central booking before morning. You'll have your mugshot taken, and you'll officially be charged with the murders of the four girls as soon as the courts open up in the morning. There's just nothing I can do to stop that from happening, and I truly apologize about that.

"The best I can do is go over everything that we talked about tonight with my supervisor in the morning. Hopefully, he will feel the same way I do about all of it, and he can make a call to the district attorney and let them know we think the wrong man is behind bars. But with what you've given us, we at least now have our noses on the scent of the killer. Though it may still be some time before we can figure out who this person is. Keep your head up, be safe, and don't mouth off to anybody. I'd hate to see something happen to you as you wait to get released."

Defeated, his head fell into his palms as the sounds of sobbing once again filled the room. I felt for him. I really did. But like I said, it was out of my hands. We just had to trust that the legal system did its job correctly and that me and Cole could find the person who was really responsible.

I gave Diamond a nudge, letting him know it was time to take our leave. I didn't look back at the kid for fear of my emotions getting the better of me. The sounds of his whimpering followed us back out onto the outside pathway between buildings.

I, for one, was ready to call it a night. I sent Diamond back into the main office outbuilding to talk with Scheffler as I made my way back to the car. Looking at my watch, I saw it was already past midnight. So much for a cozy date night with Sarah.

***

"So whatcha think?" Diamond asked as he finally got into the car twenty minutes after I had left him.

"I think the kid's telling us the truth. He had no clue that the card was missing when we asked him where it was. Why would he cop to trying to steal it if he didn't even know it was missing. That spoke volumes to me."

"What do we do now?"

"Go home, get some sleep, and try to get ahead of this thing tomorrow."

"How do you mean?"

"For starters, I'm gonna call Jack first thing and have him use his connections to see if someone has recently sold a Babe Ruth card within a three-hundred-mile radius of the District. As for you, I want you to call over to Howard the moment you wake up and see if they don't keep fingerprint files for all of their employees. If they do, I want those on my desk by the time I get in."

"Why Howard? That seems pretty specific."

"You heard what the kid said. That the ex would get fired if his relationship with the girl got out. She's not from these parts. She probably doesn't know too many people around town. So that leads me to believe that it's a teacher from her school, or a politician. Since the crime happened on campus, I deduct that someone from the school is the most likely suspect. See where I'm going with this?"

"Yes. I do now, Max. I never would've put two and two together. How'd you come up with that so quickly?"

"Years and years of doing the job, kid. You'll get there one day too, Cole, I promise. But that's enough talk about this for one night. I already had my date night ruined by this and I probably won't get any sleep tonight either, so let's put it out of our brains until tomorrow. There's nothing more we can accomplish tonight."

"Sounds good, boss."

"Oh, and one more thing before I forget. Good job in there tonight, Cole. I mean it. You were Johnny on the spot with your questions. You asked the right things at exactly the right time. It reminded me of how Jack and I used to do things. Keep it up, kid. I think there's a future detective in there just raring to come out."

Diamond's grin was the biggest I had ever seen it after my comments. I don't think he wanted to ruin it with a formal thank you. That's fine by me. I'm not one to get all mushy over stuff like that with my partner, anyway. His smile was thanks enough.

We drove the rest of the way in silence. But just as I had imagined, my brain refused to let go. I was going to be in for a long and restless night.

BaLTImore, MD
December 22nd, 3:45 AM

The street was dark and quiet when he pulled up outside of the hobby shop on the outskirts of downtown Baltimore. The man he had spoken to the night before said there would be plenty of parking in the rear of the store, but he wanted to be in and out as quickly as possible, so he parked on the street right out front.

Drop off the card and grab the cash, is what he told himself. No idle chitchat, and absolutely no mention of how he got the baseball card.

As he looked at his watch, he saw that he still had three more hours until the store would open up for the day. Not enough time to get a motel room—but too much time to sit and wait comfortably at the same time—so he took the business owner's advice and circled around the block so he could park in the rear. At least in the back he wouldn't look as suspicious if a cop on patrol saw him idling out front on the street. Especially since his rusted out 1940 Ford sedan stuck out like a sore thumb.

He pulled out the baseball card from his pocket and finally took in the beauty that the small piece of cardboard had to offer. A perfect and pristine painted image of The Sultan of Swat, baseball bat on its signature back swing, resting on the man's shoulder. His face drawn as if he was admiring one of his mammoth shots disappear over the right field wall at Yankee Stadium. He could now see what all the fuss was about. This card was not only a relic but also a snapshot of the American Dream.

The fact that an orphaned kid from the streets of Baltimore could become the great American hero that he became was what kept kids up at night. And what kept them going back to the fields or the alleys—or wherever else kids congregated—so they could team up and play the great game of baseball. At a young age, every kid thinks that they can grow up to become the next Babe Ruth. Even the colored kids. But that dream had faded for him now. As he looked at the card in his hands, he knew that the only dream he had left in his life was to sell this thing as quickly as he could and escape the country that he had called home for his entire life.

His new dream was now called survival. And in order to survive, he needed to run.

Run faster than Babe Ruth had ever even thought about.

ArLINGTON, VA

December 22nd, 1:04 AM

Sarah was sleeping soundly by the time I walked back in through the front door of my house. It was one in the morning, after all, and I wished I was lying there asleep next to her. Knowing that I would probably disturb her by climbing into the bed, I took off my shoes, my jacket and my hat, and decided to lie down on the couch instead.

Sleep never came. Maybe I drifted in and out for an hour or so, if even that. My mind was moving faster than a hamster's legs while running on its play wheel, so no real rest was had. I gave up after a while and sat up. If my mind was going to be working in overdrive, I might as well take note of what it's got to say.

Being basically back at square one was a troubling thought, but I had come back from farther in the past, so I didn't let it get to me too much.

The thing that held my attention the most was the fact that I had inadvertently kept my partner out of the loop for the second time today. I had completely forgotten to tell him about the letters that

Sarah thought she had seen drawn in blood back at the crime scene. Not that we had gotten any names from the kid at the lockup to chase down, anyway.

As my mind often does in the middle of the night, it had me now on a wild goose chase for what those letters might mean. To me, this seemed like a message; Ruby-Sue Daniels was trying to tell us who killed her and her friends.

I grabbed a few pieces of scrap paper out of one of the drawers from my desk, a pen, and I sat to write my thoughts. Jack always said this was a waste of time, but it always seems to help me visualize what we have in a case. Names, weapons, locations, alibis, etc.... it's just a whole hell of a lot easier to see it all when it's all laid out in front of me. And it's broken more than a few cases wide open to boot, so why change what isn't broken is what I say.

With no names of interest to write down, I went straight to the letters that were supposedly written in blood. I wrote down MRE on top of one page and stared at it for a while. Even though my thoughts were racing, my mind was mush at this hour. Stumped, I got up and went to the kitchen for a glass of water.

Recalling what Jimmy Malone had said about the question mark painting brought the image front and center to my mind all of a sudden as I walked to the kitchen for my water. I kept thinking of the letters MRE over and over again, too. Which then set my mind off on another tangent. One that might be more of a case breaking clue than anything else we have seen yet.

Back at the table with my pen back in hand, I put a period before the letter E and stared at the paper some more. Instead of just three random letters, they now formed a name, it seemed. As my eyes glazed over, getting fuzzy from staring at the page, I realized saying it as Mister E sounded a lot like the word mystery. Which was exactly what both Jimmy Malone and the gal from the admissions office had called Ruby-Sue's unknown ex-boyfriend. They both said that he was some sort of mystery man.

As I wracked my brain for all the names we had come across over the past thirty-six or so hours, it finally became clear to me. We were looking for one person. One that we had met just this morning. Or I guess it was yesterday morning—but regardless—I zeroed in on that one person. One that seemed to be in an awful hurry to end our chance meeting once we were introduced as detectives. Mr. Embry. The student-teacher back at Howard university. Mr. E. Not MRE.

Shit, I muttered to myself. We were face to face with the man we were looking for just this morning, and I let him walk away. Even at the insistence of Diamond that we talk to him, I waived him off as unimportant. But I think now that he is the exact person we've been looking for the entire time. His profession fit one that would put a person's job in jeopardy if they were caught fraternizing with a student. And his name surely fit the fact that Ruby-Sue's friends all called him the mystery man. Maybe they got that name from her, herself. Being how his initials sound a whole lot like the word "mystery." And then there was the question mark painted onto her bedroom wall. It was all becoming clear to me now.

Without even looking at the clock, I walked back into the kitchen and picked up the receiver of the phone off of the wall and called Diamond. I wanted him to focus his fingerprint mission on one man in the morning. His phone rang and rang and rang with no answer.

Dejected, but not defeated, I dialed another number.

"Hello?" a sleepy and grumpy Jack growled as he picked up his telephone. No memorized business greeting this time. I knew I had woken him up from a sound sleep.

"Jackie Boy, I've got a possible name for you to track down for me. Mr. Embry. Teacher at Howard University. I think this is the ex-boyfriend of the vic I was telling you about earlier."

"Gee, Maxey. Don't you think this could've waited until the morning? It's four AM right now. Don't you know a fella my age has got to get some sleep whenever he can?"

"I do apologize about the timing of the call, Jack, but this is important. One more thing for you to do first thing when you get up too, please. Get on the horn with every pawn shop, hobby shop, comic book shop, or anywhere else where collectibles might be bought and sold. Be on the lookout for a Babe Ruth card that has been sold over the past couple of days. We find that seller, we find the killer. And if I were a bettin' man, my money is on this Mr. Embry as both."

"Will do, Maxey. Now let me get back to bed so I can be up as soon as these stores raise their shutters for the day."

"Keep in touch, Jack. And once again, sorry for the hour of the call. Oh, be sure to check out stores in Virginia and Maryland, too. This guy could already be on the run."

"Aye-aye. Now go to bed!"

I took his cue as one that was needed. I had been going nonstop for close to twenty-four hours now. Even when a clue of this magnitude arises, I can't do my job if I'm sleep-walking my way through work. Jack was right. I needed sleep.

Once I was horizontal on the couch, feet up on a throw pillow on the opposite end, head under one on this side, I slept the sleep of the dead.

ArLINGTON, VA

December 22nd, 8:09 AM

I awoke to the aroma of a fresh pot of coffee brewing and the clanging of dishes being washed in the kitchen sink.

Feeling somewhat refreshed, I took a glance at the clock on the wall over the fireplace mantel and saw it was only a few minutes past eight in the morning. I maybe got four hours of sleep, but what little sleep I did get seemed to give me the recharge I was looking for. My neck was a little sore from sleeping on the couch. Even so, the short nap seemed to do wonders for my mind. It seemed as sharp as ever and ready to get back at it.

I'm not due into the station until noon on most days, but with the clues that I had uncovered last night still fresh in my mind, I didn't see the point of waiting four more hours to go into work. Not when this Embry fella was probably already on the run.

I smiled at Sarah as I joined her in the kitchen. I poured myself a cup of coffee and grabbed her from behind to give her an embrace and a kiss on the back of her head—my way of saying good morning to the woman I hoped to spend the rest of my life with. The familiarity of the situation told my mind that I could definitely get used to this. The life of a bachelor had run its course, and I was fully ready to become domesticated once again.

As I was getting ready to hit the shower and start packing my notes from last night into my briefcase, Sarah asked me if I wanted some breakfast. Not wanting to let her down again after our failed dinner date attempt from the night before, I nodded as I headed into the bathroom and shut the door behind me.

Breakfast was one meal that I had replaced with a few swallows of booze after the wife left—and I still haven't gotten back into the habit of eating before leaving for work on most days. Even though the drinking had diminished, my body still hadn't gotten back to some of the pre-divorce customs that I once had enjoyed.

With my face full of shaving foam and razor in hand, I heard the telephone ring through the closed door of the bathroom. Hoping that Jack had come across something useful, I wrapped myself in a towel and rushed out to the kitchen to answer it. Not used to having someone available to answer my phone, I got confused by only hearing two rings until I rounded the corner and heard Sarah speaking to someone on the other end. I gave her a look of surprise, seeing as how we were supposed to be keeping our relationship a secret.

"Hold on, here he comes now," she said while handing me the receiver. "It's Jack," she whispered as I took control of the phone, wiping the side of my face with a napkin that was on the table. Trying my best to not get the shaving foam that was covering my face all over the mouthpiece of the telephone.

"Jackie Boy. Watcha got for me?" I asked, pleased that my old partner had come through with something only a few hours after the request I had made to him.

"Well, good morning to you too, Maxey. Have a little company this morning, I see?" he said sarcastically.

He chuckled. I stayed silent. I was not in the mood for small talk. And I was definitely not in the mood to discuss my personal life at this hour of the morning, especially when there was a killer on the loose. Luckily, he didn't press the issue.

"I ain't havin' much luck yet tracking anything down," he continued, after realizing I wasn't taking the bait. "I talked to half a dozen collectibles outfits already this morning, none of which has seen any Babe Ruth cards recently. Though they have all asked me to call them back once we track it down. Seems that this card is pretty expensive. Probably worth more than you or I make in an entire year."

"That's what the kid I talked to last night seemed to think. Which was why he was trying to lift it. Said the money he could fetch for it was life changing," I said, momentarily thinking about what I would do with that kind of cash. But that's a pipe dream. Taking the easy money is never a guarantee. Especially not when it's taken in the circumstances that we were navigating at the moment.

"Sounds like all these other guys agree, too. So watcha want me to do now, then? Keep looking?"

"Absolutely. Have you figured out this guy's first name yet? Or his address, or anything else that might be useful to us?" I asked. Thinking it probably sounded like I was asking Jack to do our jobs for us to Sarah—who was watching keenly from the other side of the table. But knowing Jack, this was probably the happiest he's been since his retirement.

"No, I figured you wanted me to get started on a paper trail of the card first. I'll get to that this afternoon."

"No need. We'll probably have it before then. Diamond and I are gonna head back to Howard as soon as I get into the city. We've got fingerprint cards to match up with their employment records. Let's just hope there's not more than one Embry on their staff."

"You'll let me know what ya find out?"

"Of course I will. That's a stupid question, Jackie Boy," I said in a condescending tone, not meaning anything by it, but letting him know I wanted desperately to get off the phone. Not before I pressed the issue of looking beyond the city limits first, though. "But anyway. Did you reach out to any stores in Virginia or Maryland yet? My money is on this guy getting as far away from here as possible. Probably already hopped the state line. Could be on a ship to London already, far as I know."

"Not yet. Still trying to get my hands on the yellow pages for those areas. Gonna hit up a library and see if they don't have them as soon as I get off the phone here with you. But I agree. I think looking in town is a long shot. But, I gots to start somewhere. I'll be in touch."

"Thanks Jack. I'm gonna talk to McFweed and let him know I'm employing your services so you can get an invoice ready for him."

"I appreciate that, Maxey. You know I'd do this for free, but if I'm gonna have to drive a few hours to chase this guy, I'm gonna need some sort of scratch to get me back and forth. Let me know what he says. I'll leave a message at the station if anything pops up. Talk at you soon."

"Thanks, Jack," I said while standing back up, trying not to trip over the long, coiled cord that somehow had gotten tangled up between my legs.

"Hey, hon?" I asked Sarah as she was back at the stove, finishing up with the plating of our breakfast dishes. "What time you heading in this morning?"

"Oh, probably as soon as we're done with breakfast. Why?"

"Think I can snag a ride? I had a breakthrough last night and want to get a jump on this right away."

"Of course. Under one condition, though."

"And what would that be?" I asked quizzically, a smile creeping up at the corners of my mouth.

"You wipe that ridiculous white stuff off of your face first," she replied with a laugh.

I had forgotten I still even had it on my face, to be honest. I probably looked like a fool sitting there awaiting my bacon and eggs.

After going back into the bathroom and finishing my botched shave job, I rang Diamond once again. I asked him to pick up the fingerprint cards and meet me at Howard University. Since I'd be hitching a ride from Sarah, I knew that I'd be at the campus before him.

Back at the table, we ate in silence. Not for any reason I could think of other than the fact that we seemed to be content enough to enjoy each other's company to ruin it with talk of work. But that ultimately got my mind going in a weird direction. I realized that if we didn't have work to talk about, we usually didn't do much talking.

My face must've given myself up.

"What's wrong, Max? Don't you like your eggs? I added milk and cheese to them before I scrambled them, just like you like it."

"No, it's not that. It's just this case," I said, lying my ass off. I didn't want to get into what Jack always called my self-destruction mode. "The eggs are great!"

"What happened? A few minutes ago you were raring to go," she said, knowing she had me dead to rights caught up in a fib. "I know the look you get when you're about to make a breakthrough, and this isn't it. Wanna try again?"

"It's nothing, doll face, really. I'm just worried that we'll have to call in J. Edgar's boys if this guy jumped state lines. And you know how I feel about that schmuck," which wasn't a lie at all. I hated having to concede any investigation to the feds, just like the rest of my coworkers did too. Despite that, I couldn't shake the feeling that was implanted in my brain from a moment earlier. Did we actually have anything in common besides our work?

I shook it off, smiled, and continued, "but if I'm able to get McFweed to hire on Jack, then he can do our dirty work for us if this guy flees to Maryland or Virginia. Or even Europe, if he gets that far."

"Well, at least you'll get your wish then," she offered without elaborating her meaning.

"And what wish is that?"

"Your wish to work one more case with Jack," she revealed with a thoughtful smile, making me rethink the dread that was going through my mind of us not having anything in common.

I let that thought ponder as I finished my eggs. She was right about the Jack part, though. Dead on, in fact. At least this time I knew that this could be the last time I worked alongside my mentor. Unlike on our last case, where his retirement was sprung on me right before we caught the killer.

Maybe that's why I had been so reluctant to work with Diamond. Self-doubt is always apparent no matter what profession you're in. But it's amplified ten fold when you are tasked with potentially saving the lives of countless victims.

I took my plate to the sink, rinsed it off, gave Sarah a kiss on the cheek, and retrieved the clothes I was going to change into. Funny how your mind can take you in so many different places in a matter of moments. One random thought has the impact of souring your entire mood in the blink of an eye.

I was told as a rookie to never take your work home with you. Today though, I would have to be careful not to take my home life with me into the office. Not that there was really any danger of losing

Sarah—at least I hope there isn't—but once my mind gets caught up on something, it's hard to shake it. No matter how minor it is.

But I don't have time to worry about that. I have a killer to catch.

Whatever this is, it will have to wait.

Central Booking, Washington D.C.

December 22nd 10:48 AM

Jimmy returned to his cell after getting booked on four separate murder charges by the judge at the downtown courthouse. His trial in all four cases was set to begin in April 1951. He knew that if Detective Denver didn't keep his word that he would most likely be looking at the death penalty.

Denver was right though, the jail at central booking was crowded. Nothing at all like the small cell he occupied over at Howard. He currently shared a cell with seven other inmates. The worst part of that was, there were only two bunk bed style cots in the room.

Luckily for him, this small cell only served as a holding cell for prisoners either waiting to see the judge, or awaiting transport back to whatever prison it was that was holding them. For Jimmy, he had no clue where home was now.

He, of course, was not granted bail. Most colored prisoners weren't. It didn't help his case that the job he held wasn't considered worthy enough by the judge, since he worked only for tips and spare change from the customers at the diner. With no real income, and only his friend Boyd as his support system, the judge deemed him a flight risk and banished him to jail to await his trial.

His public defender didn't seem to be optimistic about the outcome of a trial and said he was going to try to work out a plea deal to get his sentence reduced in some way. Jimmy knew that to mean that they would probably take the death penalty off the table, but he would most likely still be shipped off to Alcatraz or San Quentin to spend the rest of his days.

He longed for any word whatsoever from the detectives he spoke to last night. Anything at all from them would be a blessing. Jimmy kept hoping that they would keep their word and get him out of this mess. As he looked around him, eying the scum of the earth that was surrounding him, he broke down and cried.

It was right then and there that he got down on his knees in front of God and the other prisoners in his cell and promised he would do right by Ruby-Sue and clean up his act. Starting now, he said to himself, as God as my witness. I will walk the straight and narrow path He provides for me.

One by one, the other prisoners were led away—off to their court appearances—until he was the last man in the cell. With the room's population dwindling, Jimmy retreated to an open bunk and continued to cry and pray. Small comforts such as this weren't the norm in a county jail cell. Jimmy took it as a sign, and repeated his prayer from a moment ago, again and again and again, until those words were the only thing left in his mind.

Exhaustion finally set in after a time, shutting off his consciousness until his body fell numb into a blissful sleep. It was at that moment when she came to him. Once he was mentally free of the shackles of the world around him. She didn't say anything at first, she just smiled that smile that he used to say he would die for. The same smile that she flashed him on that day at the diner when their paths first crossed. The one that made him fall head over heels for her.

The course of their entire two-week relationship played out in his mind while he slept. All of the great times the two had shared was available to him on a slow motion playback loop. The dream was so vivid that he could actually feel her touch when she embraced him as she sat on her bed and showed him the Babe Ruth card. "I forgive you," was all she said as her body morphed into a white dove and flew away.

The sound of the flapping from her tiny wings jolted him awake. The happiness vanished into the sky with her. One look at his surroundings brought back the vision of his current hell. He started to pray again, this time adding an additional promise. One that he knew for sure would get an answer to his prayer.

Within a matter of moments—as if God himself had laid his ruling down on the courthouse—a prison guard neared the cell. "Inmate Malone, come with me please," he said, while fixing the giant key into the lock of the jail cell.

Jimmy was at a loss, not knowing where he was being led to, but he followed along anyway. Anything had to be better than being cooped up with all of these strangers in that small jail cell. "You are free to go, Mr. Malone. Seems like all of your charges have been dropped."

Jimmy's jaw nearly hit the floor as he embraced the prison guard in the tightest hug he had given anyone since the last time he saw his late mother.

The guard shoved him off, probably worried that his coworkers had seen him in an embrace with a colored man. After regaining his composure and making sure to let Jimmy know that he was the man in charge, he finally led him to the entrance of the jail, handed him a paper bag full of his belongings, and opened the front door. Releasing Jimmy out into the free world once again.

Though it had only been a little less than forty-eight hours since he first entered the police station at Howard, Jimmy felt like he had spent a lifetime behind those bars. Not wanting to go back on his word to God, he took a bus home and got together a plan to improve his life. Though it wouldn't come overnight, he didn't want to waste any time. He was a new man, and he saw the world as something positive for the first time in his life. The color of his skin be damned. He was going to make a difference in this world or die trying.

Howard University

December 22nd 10:02 AM

An hour later, I was sitting on a bench outside of the admissions office on the campus of Howard University. I was flipping through my notes from the night before—seeing if I had anymore epiphanies up my sleeve—while patiently awaiting the arrival of my partner. I saw a few people milling around in the courtyard—coming and going from doors that led to the various buildings—like today was just another day. But other than those few people, the campus was quiet.

Any signs of impact from the quadruple murder that had taken place on these grounds a few days prior was now nonexistent. Not that the campus was buzzing with a stir or anything, but the somberness seemed to be gone from the few faces that I did see.

I wondered if word had gotten out to any of the people who were away for their Christmas break yet. Or even if there would be another mourning period when the students would reconvene for the first day of class in a few weeks. Surely this had to have made the national news.

But then again, who knows? These were four colored girls we were talking about, and news of cases like these often got swept under the carpet. The press tries their best to not upset the white folks these days, so we probably won't see any headlines as bold as "Four Negros Slain in Washington" in any of the national rags anytime soon.

Regardless of all of that, I have this Embry fella on my radar now, and it won't be long until I've got my hooks in him. Especially now that I've got the services of Jack Barnaby, Private Eye, on my side. He's able to cross state lines and investigate freely now that he's not behind the badge. There's nowhere this Embry guy can go that I can't reach him.

Though I doubted I would see him on campus today, my eyes were on high alert for the man we were looking for. He was long gone by now. I knew it in my bones. I also knew that nothing would stop me from tracking him down and bringing him in like the rabid animal that he appeared to be.

There's no doubt in my mind that the prints on the card that Diamond was bringing from the station would be an exact match to the prints that the school had on file. We will have him dead to rights after that. Only thing left to do will be to track him down, haul him in and hand him over to the courts. The judge and jury will then decide if he fries in the chair or gets sent to The Rock.

Impatient from sitting idle for too long on the bench, I took one more look around my surroundings before starting off towards the doors of the admissions office like a man on a mission. Hopefully Diamond will know where to find me. I can't just sit here and wait, not when there are answers to be found beyond that set of double doors that stand in front of me.

"Hello, Miss Watson," I said as I entered through the admissions office doors. The heat from the furnace felt nice on my face, as the wind had been whipping its cold breeze across my body as I sat and waited outside. "I'm Detective Denver. We spoke a couple of days ago. I don't know if you remember me or not."

"Yes, I remember you. It's not every day that the police come to visit me at work. How could I ever forget a meeting like that?" She said with a nervous laugh. One that immediately brought a bout of suspicion to my forefront, though ultimately, I chalked it up to her nerves. People often get nervous in our company, and she was no different. If Ms. Watson were somehow involved in this mess, she would've been long gone by now.

"Yes, well, I'm hoping you can help me out today. I gots me a couple of follow-up questions about someone on staff here," I stated, hoping that I might calm her nerves a bit if she knew I wasn't there to interrogate her. "My partner should be along soon with a fingerprint card of some prints that we took from the residence. We'd like to try to match them up with a person of interest. And, if it's not too much trouble, we'd also like to take a look at the employment records of Mr. Embry."

A laugh escaped through her pursed lips. One of both humor and doubt, it seemed. Like I was a fool for even bringing up the name Mr. Embry to her. "You think Horace had something to do with this?" She said through the laugh.

"Horace?" I asked. Not familiar with that name.

"Yes. Horace Embry. That's who you're asking about, right?"

"If that's the man you introduced us to the other day, then yes, that is exactly who I'm asking about. Is he in by any chance?" I asked, knowing full well that he was most likely miles away from campus at this moment in time. But it never hurts to ask the stupid questions. Ever. Especially not after I let the man off the hook last time we were here. I'm not making that same mistake twice.

"No, he's not in today. As a matter of fact, I haven't seen him since the last time you were here. Funny. Now that you ask about him, he was acting kinda strange the rest of that day."

"Strange, how?" I asked.

"He seemed to be flustered. He was dropping his paperwork all throughout the office. Fumbling his keys..." she paused, trying to make it all make sense in her mind, "and strange stuff like that. Not acting like the suave man that we all know and love at all. I knew he had tutored Ruby-Sue in the past with her algebra homework, so I figured he was just upset that she was gone. Maybe the two of them had become friends outside of classwork, or something like that. But this whole year, up until yesterday, he had never missed a day of work without notice. Yet, here we are—two days in a row, now—that he hasn't come in and hasn't left word with anybody about why he wasn't able to come to work," she tailed off into silence as the severity of the situation seemed to hit her full force.

Seemed like my suspicions of the man were proving to be true. I almost wanted to ask for his address and book it over to his house right then. But I had to wait for Diamond. Though his fingerprint card seemed like a moot point by now. Embry was definitely the man we were looking for. Nothing spells out guilt more than acting strange in the one place you should feel the least threatened.

"Do you think you can get me his employment records? I would like to have a look at them, if you don't mind. I think it would be foolish on our part not to have a stop by his house, especially after all of this talk of his unexcused absence from the office."

"Ya. Sure. I'll go and grab them," she said with a look of sadness. Seems like the gravity of the situation involving her coworker was finally hitting home for her. "Gimme a minute. They keep the records in the filing cabinets in the other room. If you'll have a seat, I'll be back with them in a few minutes."

As soon as Ms. Watson walked down the hallway, I felt a whoosh of wind come up behind me as I turned to see Cole walk in through the doors from the outside. The cool breeze gave me flashbacks from my time spent shivering on the bench out there waiting for him a few moments ago. I could sense he was upset about me not waiting for him like I said I would, so I tried to defuse the situation before it fully arose.

"Embry hasn't been in since we were here last," I said as Diamond took a seat next to me. I handed him my notes from the night before, as well as the photographs that Sarah had given me from when I had the epiphany that the letters MRE actually spelled out Mr. E. He hadn't yet seen the photos, so I had to catch him up to speed quickly. From the look on his face, I could tell that he was confused, but this was one of those moments where the look on my face protested and said, "trust me."

"Looks like he's definitely our man," I continued after Cole looked through the pictures and notes. "Ms. Watson is fetching his employment records right now. Should give us an address for him, though I'd bet ten bucks that he's already on the run. I've got Jack looking into any businesses that deals in sports memorabilia, so hopefully he gets a hit on that soon. I don't think we even need to worry about matching his prints. Even she said he was acting strange that day. He's guilty as sin, you ask me."

"So, you just want me to sit on the prints, then?" Diamond asked. "I get your point, but isn't it protocol to make sure we have the right guy?"

"We've got the right guy, Colio, no doubt about that," I said frankly. "Ms. Watson said that Embry used to tutor Daniels. Maybe those sessions turned into a romance. Makes sense why she couldn't tell her friends who he was. The whole thing adds up. This is our guy. Besides, there will be plenty of time to match fingerprints later. Like when he's booked for killing those four girls."

"Alright, if you say so, Max," he said, as his words didn't seem to add up with his thoughts. "I just wish you'd keep me in the loop more."

I shook my head. Here we go again.

"I rang your house last night. Right after I figured out the letters. That was the first I had seen of the photos, and you were the first phone call I made. So don't think that I'm out here doing all the work without you, kid. I called Jack second, asking him to look into those businesses for us. Because I'd be a fool not to think that this guy hasn't already jumped state lines. And you and I both know that we can't go questioning folks in Virginia or Maryland since it's out of our jurisdiction," I said in a harsh, but quiet, tone. I didn't want to alert the rest of the office that we were having a disagreement.

He stared down the same hallway that Ms. Watson had gone down a moment earlier, probably wondering if he should make a call to McFweed and rat me out for going against protocol. I don't blame him. When I was a rook, I probably would've had the exact same thoughts that he is most likely having now.

But I always followed Jack's lead. Always. Sure, we had our disagreements, but the man never steered me wrong on a case. That kind of trust will have to be learned from Diamond. No matter how many times I tell him it's in his best interest to follow my lead. He will have to figure that out on his own.

Protocol is, after all, supposed to be followed to the letter, and it's been something that I've been preaching to the kid from the moment we got our first case together. But gut feeling is a hard thing to teach.

And it's even harder to know when to listen to your gut and when to throw that advice to the wayside.

That knowledge only comes with years of experience. Which is something that I can't teach Diamond. That only comes with years and years of putting your nose to the ground and following the clues that are given to you.

This instance right now was one of those times where I knew that following protocol would only slow us down. My gut was screaming from the altars that Embry was our guy. And with the belief that this guy has probably already made a run for it, we don't exactly have the time to pour over fingerprint cards for the sake of protocol. We needed to act. Now.

Ms. Watson returned with the paperwork we were after. Diamond and I thanked her for her cooperation, letting her know we would be in touch if we needed any further assistance. Within moments, we were back outside in the cold, beating a path back to our car.

With address in hand, en route to the home of Horace Embry, I radioed McFweed and asked him for backup.

We were going to need every available cop for this one.

Brookland

December 22nd, 11:39 AM

Embry lived a few miles away from campus in a nice part of town. Well, nice enough that you didn't need to worry about locking your doors. Though since it was still a predominantly colored part of town, most people did anyway.

His front door was only mere feet from the street—with no driveway to speak of—so we parked haphazardly in front of the house. Diamond and I walked around the corner to the small alley where parking spaces were allotted for this row of houses. The line of police vehicles that had followed us took up most of the street, blocking traffic in both directions. This was strategically done, leaving fewer options for a person to flee if it came to that.

We didn't try to hide ourselves. Lights were flashing and sirens were blaring the whole way. The convoy of seven vehicles alerted the entire neighborhood to our presence. By the time the last car threw on their parking brake, the sidewalks on both sides of the street were full of curious eyeballs. It's not a sight uncommon to us. The old adage 'curiosity killed the cat' doesn't seem to apply to folks when they see the red and blue lights start to flash.

Ignoring the hoopla that seemed to follow us down the alley, I made my way to the rear door of the residence. We learned from his employment records that Embry drove a dark brown 1940 Ford sedan. An additional comment stated that the car's paint had eroded with rust so badly that it could actually be any color underneath. And as I had imagined, no such car was anywhere to be found out on the street or in the back alley. But with the description of the car that we had; it gave me hope that it wouldn't be too hard to track down. There can't be that many cars in such disarray here in the District, which reminded me of the car I saw tearing out of the alley the other night. That couldn't be a coincidence.

Undeterred, I pounded my fist on a wooden door that looked like it could use a fresh coat of paint. White flecks flew into the afternoon sun from the impact of my knocking. The windows next to the door shook with panic from the vibrations my thumping produced, sending dirt and dust into the surrounding air from the screen that reverberated off of the glass.

"Horace Embry," I shouted. "We have the place surrounded. Come out with your hands up and nobody has to get hurt."

I looked behind me to see if I had the backup I needed. Four other sets of eyes besides Diamond's were on the door, ready and waiting for my call to breach.

Diamond and I looked to be underdressed for the occasion, as we were the only two men in jackets and ties. The rest were outfitted with their batons at the ready, shotguns slung over their shoulders, and one man had a handheld battering ram, ready to explode the door from its frame when given the go ahead.

I waited for a count of ten before shouting again, "Horace Embry, this is the Metropolitan Police Department! Come out with your hands up or we will be forced to gain entry."

This time I waited a full fifteen count with my right fist clenched tight in the air, signaling the officers behind me to wait for my command. With still no answer, I gave the sign. I stepped back and watched as the battering ram turned the old wooden door into splinters as it came loose from its hinges and opened up in front of us. The sound of metal crushing wood was deafening under the canopy of the eave.

Taking another step back, I allowed the other officers to make first entry, holding my arm out to stop Diamond from following in behind the rushing men. Once my arm had stopped his forward momentum, I whispered, "hold up a sec, Cole. Let them clear the house first."

He nodded and fell back. I could see the adrenaline coming off of him. His eyes fixed on the door ahead of him with as much clarity as one of the hopheads we come across in the parks late at night. A door slammed inside, and poor Cole jumped as though it were a gunshot instead.

Situations like these are ones that the academy can never truly train you for. When the prospect of danger lurks around the corner of an open door, only your primal senses can fully prepare you. It's then up to your brain to realize which mode you should take, fight or flight. Once you get that shot of adrenaline into your bloodstream though, every lesson you've learned at the academy is as good as gone.

A few long moments later, the officer with the battering ram came back out to let us know the house was clear. I hadn't realized it, but I had my piece trained straight ahead at the empty door frame as he came out. Second nature takes over after a time, I guess. Good thing my nerves weren't as high as Diamond's, or we'd have another dead body on our hands.

The coppers inside the house didn't cause too much damage in their search. The place still looked pretty well organized and put together as we walked in. Though it was dark because of the curtains all being closed, we could still see from the light that snuck through the cracks and through the broken back door. I didn't know what we were looking for other than Embry or anything that made it look like he took off and wasn't coming back.

I made my way through each room, quickly scanning the spaces for any clues as to where he might be. There were some plates left in the sink from a meal that didn't look to be too old—as well as a stocked refrigerator—making it seem like someone was coming back home. That thought stuck with me for a moment until I went into the bedroom. A closet looked to have been ransacked. Possibly from the perp trying to scrounge together a getaway bag. That's when reality sunk in. The guy was gone. And we were none the wiser to where he might have fled to. Having seen enough, I headed back out.

"Whatcha think?" McFweed asked as he saw me rounding the corner and making a beeline straight for him.

"The place is pretty clean," I said. "Looks like he packed a bag in a hurry, though. Dresser drawers were open, and there was a lone sock on the floor by the bed. From the looks of it, I don't think he's planning on coming back."

"Makes sense. Even if he doesn't know that we're onto him, he's an educated man. It won't take him long to figure it out," McFweed said, nodding in agreement with me.

"I think he made a run for it. Which reminds me. I've got Jack looking into some businesses in Virginia and Maryland. Places where a card of this value might end up. Did he send you an invoice yet?"

"A courier dropped it off about an hour ago. I signed off on it immediately," he said while clapping his hand on my shoulder. I think that's his way of saying 'good job.' "That was smart thinking, Denver. At least it lets us keep tabs on this guy without alerting the feds to the case yet."

"I agree. The longer we can hold off J Edgar's boys, the better. Besides, ain't they too busy rounding up Reds to get involved in something as measly as a quadruple homicide?" I said with a nervous chuckle, which McFweed met with a laugh of his own.

The laughter came from an inside joke around our department at the ineptitude of the FBI in recent years. Mainly that their focus had been on gathering communist sympathizers rather than fighting crime in our country.

The District is small. You can cross state lines without even realizing it in some parts of the city. And once that happens, it's technically federal jurisdiction. So, the longer we can keep a lid on this, the better. I just hope that Jack has some luck soon before this guy really becomes the ghost that he seemed to be less than twenty-four hours ago.

I started back for the car to fetch my briefcase. I figured McFweed should be in the loop with my findings from the night before. I gave him the rundown of my idea over the radio on our way over to the Embry house, but pictures are a lot stronger than words. Not that he doubted me. We may not see eye to eye at all times, but he's never second guessed a call I've made on a case in the past.

I picked up the radio on the dash and called into the precinct to see if any word from Jack had come through yet. Negative. Though I had a message from Ms. Watson stating that it was urgent that I get in touch with her. That got my brain flying off in about a thousand different scenarios all at once. Not one of them good, either.

Better round up Diamond and get back to the university, I thought as I headed back towards the house. Who knows how dire her message could really be? I don't want to chance it if she might have some intel on our Mr. Embry. Criminals are creatures of habit—like most individuals—so maybe he finally called in to let his employers know he would be taking a leave of absence after all. You never know what kind of outlandish things a suspect will do when they feel they can finally let their guard down. I have a feeling if he could sell off the card that the money he made from it would definitely give him a feeling of ease.

Officer's Davis and Miller were pulling up as I was walking back to the front of the house, ready to start their watch command of the property. I didn't envy those two at all. They would most likely spend the next eight hours fielding questions from the neighbors and hearing outlandish claims about how they all knew that Embry was a man to keep an eye on.

Though I bet just yesterday, each and every one of them would've stuck up for him if their lives depended on it. Neighborhoods form a tight bond in this city, but there's no bond tighter than in a colored neighborhood. That community sticks by one another like no other. Not that I blame them. If the police and politicians don't have their backs, who else will if not their neighbors?

I spotted Diamond bumping gums with one of the officers who breached the house with us. I gave him a wave as I approached McFweed to fill the lieutenant in on the memo I had just received. I motioned him over, letting him know it was time to head out.

"What gives, Max?" Diamond asked as he approached me and McFweed.

"Just got word that we're needed back at Howard. Ms. Watson has something for us. Let's pack it up. There's nothing more for us to do here, anyway. Besides, those two dingbats Davis and Miller are here to take up their post. Embry ain't coming back here. You can count on that."

I left my notes and photographs with McFweed and headed back to the car. For once, my gut was silent.

I don't know if that's a good thing or a bad thing yet.

Baltimore, MD

December 22nd, 7:13 AM

Ten thousand dollars was the most money he had ever seen before. The wad that the man behind the counter of Willie's Hobby Shop gave him for the Babe Ruth card would hardly fit in his pocket. Even with the multiple rubber bands he put around it to suppress its bulge, he still had a hard time cramming it into his jeans. It was more than enough money to pay off the rest that he owed on his house, with some left over to trade in his old jalopy and get a new set of wheels.

But that wasn't in the cards for him. No. Not today, at least. Maybe once he flees the country, he'll have enough to start over. He can buy a new house or a car then, but that was still a long way away. First, he needed to find his way out.

Find a way out of this city first and foremost, and then out of the country. That was his ultimate goal, but he knew it wouldn't take long for the law to put the pieces together. Especially now that he had missed a couple of days of work. The fuzz would be after him sooner rather than later, giving him less time to concoct the perfect escape.

The airport was his first idea, but he figured they would plaster his name and face throughout every airport from here all the way down to Georgia. That wouldn't work. Not if he wanted to get the chance to enjoy his newfound riches, at least.

The bus system could get him out of Maryland quickly, but then what? He would still have to worry about being spotted at an airport in another city, too.

Then he thought of heading south. Mexico was too far south to take a bus. Probably a three-day ride at the least, he thought. Though he would probably have no problems crossing the border there. A lot less trouble than crossing into Canada, but that's where he thought the cops would look for him, so he needed another plan. All he knew was that he needed to get out of Baltimore in a hurry.

He started due west instead. The California sunshine would be a nice place to spend the rest of his life. He could change his name and fit in there without a problem, he thought. It was far enough away that the local cops from the District wouldn't bother him and his new life. There's no way they would come looking for him out in L.A. But he needed a plan. Driving across the county hellbent on finding a new life wasn't enough. He needed a place to lie low for a bit. A place to hide out and let the heat die off of his trail.

That's when he remembered the place his family had gone to on vacation when he was a boy. His father saved up all year to take his family to the river. They went there summer after summer for what seemed like his entire youth. A place where he was more than familiar with. A place that would be deserted at this time of the year too: the campground at Great Falls, Virginia. Right on the banks of the Potomac River.

He could break into one of the cabins and live pretty comfortably for a few weeks while he formulated his plan. But he would need supplies. It's far too cold to be outside trying to hunt and trap his food, plus it had been more than ten years since he had skinned and cleaned a deer properly. He was going to need help, and he knew just the person who he thought would do anything for him.

That young girl who used to bat her eyelashes at him every time he walked by back at Howard.

Yes, she was just the type of person who would risk it all for him.

Just like he thought Ruby-Sue was. Until he found out she wasn't.

HOWard UNIVersITY
December 22nd, 1:45 PM

Ms. Watson came bursting out through the double doors at the first sight of us. She looked pretty frazzled, yelling frantically that Embry had called her.

"Slow down, Miss," I said in an attempt to calm her down a bit. Her words were coming out so fast that I had a hard time understanding what she was saying.

"He called me!" She screamed.

"Who did? Who called you?" I asked, knowing full well who she was talking about, but I wanted her to slow her breathing so she could speak coherently.

"Horace!" she screamed. "Horace called me. He wants me to bring him some supplies and some food. He's staying in a cabin out at Great Falls. Right up the river from here!" Tears were running down her face as she was screaming at the top of her lungs at us. "Please don't make me go see him. I don't want to end up like those other girls."

The fear in her voice and in her eyes was true. She had worked with this man day in and day out for the entire school year. She must've subconsciously known that he was capable of terrible things, even if her mind wouldn't alert the rest of her body to the dangers that he exposed.

"Calm down," I said, reaching out both of my hands to place on her upper arms to convey to her I meant her no harm. "You don't have to go anywhere you don't want to, okay? Why don't we go inside? Let's get out of this cold weather and talk about the phone call. Does that sound good?"

She nodded and mouthed the word "yes," though no noise came out of her mouth. I took her by the hand and led her back in through the same set of double doors I had entered through just a few hours prior.

"So, tell me," I started, "why do you think Horace called you? Weren't there any other people here that would want to help him?"

"I don't know," she said while wiping the tears away with a tissue that she plucked out of a box from the counter. "He said that he didn't know who else he could turn to. That I was probably the only person at the school that he could trust."

"And what did you say to that?" I asked.

"I told him I didn't think I could. That I was busy. He kept insisting that I help him." She paused, taking the tissue to her eyes once again. "I made more and more excuses why I couldn't help him, but he kept saying that I was the only person he could turn to."

"You did the right thing. I'm glad that you called us," I said, once again reaching out to hold her hands in comfort. "We can help you get through this."

"I don't think I can. I don't think I wanna be anywhere near him. I'm afraid he'll do to me what he did to the other girls."

We let her work through her thoughts and her tears on her own. Through sniffles and whimpers, she eyed the both of us, probably wondering if she was doing the right thing or not. It was three or four minutes before anyone spoke again. I was watching her face. Watching her eyes. Waiting for just the right moment before I posed my next question, but Cole beat me to it. The look I flashed him could've broken a mirror.

"Did you ask him if he did it?" Diamond asked. "Did you ask him why he killed those girls?"

There was no reason for him to know the delicate nature of the timing needed in a questioning like this. It was the first time he'd ever been in this type of situation before. I hoped it didn't ruin the best chance we were going to get to catch this guy.

"No," she said with a look of surprise. Maybe we still had a chance after all. "I didn't bring anything like that up to him. I was too afraid. He just kept telling me to promise him that I'd help. I went silent for a while. I just listened while he kept telling me to help him. This is all too much for me. I'm just a student here. I'm only twenty. I'm too young for this!"

"Did he say that he was going to be there long?" I asked, trying to keep her mind on him. The more she spoke, the less time she would have to find a way out of doing this. I knew I couldn't force her to do anything she didn't want to do, even if this was probably our only chance of getting to him. But this had to be her decision. She had to be the one that said okay.

"No," she said after a few deep breaths, trying to remember everything about the conversation she had with the man, "he didn't say. He just said he needed a few pairs of wool socks, some long Johns, and the shopping list he gave me for the grocery store seems like he'll be there at least a week."

"Let me see what you've got there," I said, wanting to take a look at the supply list he had given her. Make sure we weren't going to be walking into the trap of a man who wanted to be loaded to the gills with weapons. Even though this was only the third time I'd met her, she seemed to act on her feet. Not many other people in her situation would have thought to make a list in a situation like this. Fear normally takes over and all thought goes out the window. "Like I said before, you don't have to go anywhere you don't want to. This is all up to you. But if you agree to do this, we will be with you every step of the way, okay?"

She nodded in agreement. Deep breath after deep breath filled the silence between the three of us. I honestly didn't know which direction she was leaning. All I knew was that we needed to come up with a solution fast. Even with him waiting for her to show up with the supplies, every minute that he was out in those woods alone was more time for him to fortify his defense.

"Does he usually carry any weapons?" Diamond asked, finally breaking the deafening silence in the room. I think the severity of the situation was creeping into his forethought. Wanting to know what we were walking into if she wouldn't be our way in. "Should we put word out that an armed and dangerous man is in the area of the campground?"

She shook her head. "I've never seen him with any sort of weapon before at all, but I know he has a temper," she said in a clearer voice than before. I wondered if she was finally contemplating this after all. "Even though he was only an assistant professor, there were plenty of stories of him coming unglued in the classroom. Whacking his yard stick on the backs of students' hands, throwing baskets full of chalk in the lecture hall. That sort of thing. But I've never once seen him with a weapon on campus. Not that I've ever seen him outside of campus, though. Who knows what he's normally like?"

"The good news is, when we searched his house earlier, we didn't come across any weapons. No guns or knives, or even any boxes of ammunition lying around anywhere. There was nothing in that house that made it look like he would be the type of person to carry a gun on him," I said, trying to calm both of them down due to the direction this conversation had turned.

"Thank god for that," she replied. "I don't think I could do this if he was armed. He always seemed so nice to me, though. I couldn't imagine him using a weapon of any kind. But I guess we were all wrong about that."

Silence once again filled the room as we all three contemplated her last statement. It's never easy finding out the truth about someone you work so closely with. Especially when that truth is as brutal as his was.

"Those cabins are probably pretty bare this time of the year. But we can never be too careful," I said, wanting to make it very clear that we had no idea how far he would go. A wild animal is the most dangerous when they are cornered. And a murderer on the loose is just about as unpredictable as that. "Here's what we're going to do. You go and get all the supplies he's asking for..."

"No!" she screamed, interrupting me mid-sentence. "I won't do it!"

"Ms. Watson, you haven't even heard what I'm planning on saying. Give me that chance, and then we will both listen to your arguments. Can you do that for me, please?"

"Okay," she said in an almost inaudible voice after a short period of silence.

"You're going to run along and pick up everything that he needs. Like I said before, we will be with you all the way. Now, he's expecting you to come through for him. If you don't show up, he will know that you've turned on him and will flee at the first chance he gets. We don't want that to happen, do we?"

"No, I suppose you're right, Mr. Denver," she said as she sat up in her chair. Her tears were now dried, and she had the look of someone who wanted to do the right thing. I think my last statement finally won her over. Though I'm sure it still scared her to her wit's end.

"Now, after you get all of your supplies, Detective Diamond and I will follow you on the drive over there. Once we are about to leave, I'm going to have my lieutenant call to the authorities in Virginia to meet us there as well. I am also going to use a private investigator that we are using in this case. All of them will have orders to not make contact with him until we get there. Does that sound like something you could go along with? You will be protected by several men at all times. All of which will have eyes on the cabin from afar. There will be no chance of him hurting you. Think you could do that for us?"

"Alright," she said in the same hardly audible tone as before. Tears were welling up in her eye ducts once again. I don't know if I would've been able to go through with something of this magnitude when I was her age. She was showing more strength than I had given her credit for, that's for sure.

"Don't think of this as helping him out or helping us out," I said, giving one last attempt at reeling her in. "Think of it as helping those girls out. You can do what they couldn't. Bring justice to the man who took their lives."

"I think I can do that," she said with a nod after another long pause.

"I will do this for you as long as you can promise me I'll be safe," she said as she looked me dead in the eyes. Her fear was apparent on her face as her bottom lip quivered as she spoke.

"I promise," I vowed in return as I met her gaze, knowing full well that in my position, I was in no place to make such a promise.

This was a big ask. Maybe the biggest ask I've ever had to ask a civilian. But this was our best shot at getting this guy. Maybe even our only shot.

"How long until he expects you, do you think?" Diamond asked.

"I'm not sure. I didn't give him a definite answer. I just said okay as I hung up the phone with him."

I looked at my watch. It was already going on two in the afternoon. We didn't have much daylight left, and to be honest, our chances of bringing this guy in safely were diminishing with every minute passed. Daylight was key to this type of stakeout. Under the fall of darkness, it will be damn near impossible to pull off this type of surveillance in a deeply wooded area. The only thing that will be on our side will be the roar of the waterfall. Even with that sort of noise, getting too close, too soon, could spook him. Then who knows what measures he will go to to ensure his freedom. That was a chance I'd rather not take.

"Let's get a move on, then. Diamond, you go with Ms. Watson to gather the supplies. I'll call McFweed and Barnaby and give them the plan. Let's meet back here in an hour. We roll out at three."

"Copy that, boss," Diamond said as he followed Ms. Watson to the parking area to get into her car.

I used the administration office telephone as my gut was doing somersaults, trying its best to alert me to something. I ignored it as the phone rang on the other end. I hoped it didn't come back to haunt me.

Rural Virginia

December 22nd, 3:00 PM

With Ms. Watson's car loaded up with the supplies that Embry had asked for, we set out for the campground at three o'clock on the dot. By my estimation we would arrive right around four, giving us an hour, at best, of daylight. I didn't like cutting it this close, but it's not like we had any other options. If Watson didn't show up with the supplies, Embry would spook and most likely be on the run again. That's the exact type of outcome we needed to avoid at all costs.

McFweed phoned ahead to the local authorities in Virginia. They were sending everyone from the local deputies to the state troopers. This was probably the most action they've seen in years out there.

Jack was already en route. He hadn't had any luck tracking down the sale of the sports card, though that didn't really matter anymore. We had our guy. Or at least the location of him. And Jack will still be an integral part of us tracking him down. McFweed gave the order that the Virginia troopers were only there to assist, and that it was mine and

Diamond's collar. Even though we were outside of our jurisdiction. Let's just hope they obey their orders.

Diamond and I climbed into our car and followed Ms. Watson from a distance. Close enough to not lose her, but far enough away to not give the appearance of her having a tail. That's easy enough for right now. It's once we get to the campground is where we'll run into problems. The place is closed for the season. There should be zero cars coming or going besides the park rangers, so we will have to reconvene before going onto the property to formulate our plan with all the jurisdictions present and accounted for.

My nerves were sky high on the ride over. And I could tell that Diamond's were as well. This wasn't your average stakeout. This was about as high stakes as it could get. Knowing that I was flanked with the help of a rookie as green as a dollar bill wasn't an easy pill to swallow, either. But this will be a valuable learning opportunity for him. And at least I'll have proper backup once there. Though, depending on how Diamond pulls through in this situation, I'll know if he's suited for this job or not.

We drove in silence as every imaginable scenario played out in my mind. I had no idea what to expect out of Embry. What I did know was he was eager to get to freedom. To what extent he will go to is still up in the air. I only hope that the cabin he chose was free of any weapons. We will have the element of surprise on our side, but if he's lucky enough to fall into the possession of a hunting rifle, that all goes out the window.

The pullout to the side of the campground entrance was already full of police vehicles as we pulled up. Through the thick of the trees, I could barely see the river below. I think this will work perfectly. We should be able to send a few different groups into the trees undetected. Approaching the house with ease under the cover of the brush.

There seemed to be a never-ending mist in the atmosphere from the waterfall all around us too—making the air thicker and darker—giving us another form of camouflage that we can use to our advantage. Now I'm starting to think that the darker it is, the better it will be for us. No way we will be spotted from afar in this dense of a forest in the dark. With almost zero visibility through the trees as it is, the darkness will double our invisibility.

Besides ours and Watson's vehicles, the only other unmarked car was the pickup truck belonging to Jack, which we could use to our benefit. This way, four or five of us won't have to squeeze into Ms. Watson's car. Diamond and I can hide out in her car as she drives near the cabins while McFweed can ride with Jack, coming down the road a few minutes after we start off. The rest of the men can take to the forest trails, keeping out of sight while they maneuver into position.

By my estimation, there were over twenty uniformed officers awaiting our arrival. *Good*, I thought, we have plenty of backup.

They can flank the cabin from all sides, giving Embry even less of a chance to escape. My plan seemed to be laying out perfectly in front of me, though my gut was still twisted in knots. Something was up, but I didn't have time to figure it out.

I got out of the vehicle as the rest of the MPD convoy arrived and met McFweed as he opened his door. The roar from the nearby falls made it hard for me to hear him as he said his greeting.

Even though this was my collar, he was still the man in charge of this operation, and he let everyone know it the second he opened his mouth.

"Gentlemen," he barked as he neared the group of awaiting officers and troopers. "My name is Ted McFweed, Homicide Lieutenant, with the Metropolitan Police Department. We believe our fugitive, Horace Embry, is holed up in one of the cabins here at the campground. He asked Ms. Watson here to pick up some supplies for him. You are going to follow her in from a distance on foot through the cover of the trees. We don't want to spook him with all of our vehicles. Detective's Denver and Diamond will ride with Watson. I will be with Investigator Barnaby in his pickup truck. We still have the element of surprise on our side, and we can't afford to lose that. Any questions?"

A slew of hands flew up into the air at the end of his speech, all of which McFweed completely ignored as he walked towards Ms. Watson to make sure she was up for the next leg of her journey. Not that she had any other choice. We had all come this far already, no use chickening out now.

With everyone on the same page, McFweed gave the go ahead.

Ms. Watson turned over her engine as we watched the men head off into the woods in various directions. As the seconds passed, the last of the men finally disappeared into the thickness of the trees, seemingly out of sight to the rest of the world.

A wisp of smoke could be seen weaving its way through the trees as we drove down the bumpy dirt road, signaling which cabin it was that Embry had chosen. If the smoke from the fire he'd lit didn't give it away at first glance, the light that shone through the windows surely would to anyone who got close enough to the cabin.

Hidden in the back seat, I couldn't see my surroundings as we drove. The only thing I could see at all was Diamond's head bobbing up and down with each rut we passed over on the road. He was on the seat; I was on the floorboard. We gave Ms. Watson a clearing of a few minutes after she gathered the supplies out of her trunk before we emerged from the car. Giving her time to get everything inside and also giving the illusion that she had come alone.

I could hear the creaking of the trees as they swayed in the slight breeze that had become stronger the closer we had gotten to the falls.

The eeriness of the sounds gave me thoughts of the horror movies I used to watch as a child. Nothing good ever came from creeping around in the woods after dark in those. Hopefully, we didn't meet that same fate here tonight.

I gave Diamond a nudge, signaling to him it was go time. I held my index finger up to my lips, making sure he knew to keep it as quiet as he possibly could when exiting the vehicle. Once he was out and crouched at the back of the car, I got up and followed suit. Thinking to myself that the next time we find ourselves in this situation, I'm taking the seat, as I found it less than ideal getting up off of the floorboards gracefully.

Once outside—and finally behind the vehicle with him—we both reached for our weapons and made sure we had an extra clip at the ready, just in case it was needed. It was dark. The only light providing us any view at all was from the cabin itself. Slowly, I started the fifteen-to-twenty-yard approach to the cabin, making sure I stayed as low to the ground as possible. The front window faced the parking area of the cabin, so any sudden movement would surely stand out to the people inside.

I noticed the first of the foot soldiers approaching from the west. There were four in this group. Long rifles drawn and ready. Not a single noise coming from their direction. I don't know how they did it, marching so stealthily through the foliage of broken tree branches and leaves. Once they were in position, I made my final approach to the cabin's wall. Diamond was two steps behind me. But all was not well.

As Diamond's back hit the wall, the front door opened. We must've alerted Embry to our presence somehow. A shot rang out, hitting the side of the cabin less than two feet away from my head as Embry had emerged from the house. One of the men from the forest took a pot shot at him.

This was not at all how this was supposed to go down. At the sound of the gunshot, Embry fled into the woods towards the sound of the rushing water.

"Shit!" I screamed. "You morons let him get away!"

Great Falls, VA
December 22nd, 4:01 PM

T he sound from the gun spooked Embry. Throwing his mind into a tailspin as he rushed into the woods to find his escape.

Damn, he cursed to himself. He was in no position to defend himself in a gunfight. He knew he should have been better prepared for something like this, but he was in too much of a hurry to flee. Too busy planning his future than spending the necessary time to formulate a real plan. One that would ensure not only his survival but also one that consisted of a new life for him on the other side.

That money had changed him already. Dreams of a posh lifestyle with enough money to start over flooded his vision, proving his fears of being an amateur true. And now that money was probably gone before he even had a chance to enjoy any of it. Left inside the cabin that he would have no way of getting back to unseen. Not unless he could wait them out. But how long would that take? Days at the least. They had his scent. And they weren't going to back down now. Especially since he was on the run with nowhere to go but across the freezing waters of the Potomac.

How did they find me so fast? He asked himself as he ran from the porch and darted into the woods surrounding the cabin. It was never going to be as easy as he had drawn it up in his head. He knew that much. But he had no time to figure out his next move now, not if he wanted to survive, that is. The time for planning had passed. His only action now was to run.

Though he was somewhat familiar with the area, it had been years since he had been there. He was too busy getting a fire started and warming up the cabin to go out looking for any escape routes. A rookie mistake that he wouldn't let happen again. If he got another chance, at least. It was becoming all too clear to him that he had failed once again. An escape of this magnitude took planning. All he did was take the money and run. Quite figuratively. He was in over his head and out of options.

Through the woods he had played in as a youth, he spotted the trail that led to the water, checking back over his shoulder every few seconds to see if he had a tail as he ran. He thought about burying himself in some brush and waiting out the cavalry that was after him, but he wasn't sure if they had any dogs with them or not. If they did, he would be snuffed out no matter where he tried to hide.

He had only seen the two detectives he had met back at the university on the porch of the cabin, but since the gunshot came from the woods beyond the driveway, he knew there was probably a minimum of ten to twenty other cops looking for him too. If they split up, his hiding spots would diminish, causing him to toss out the idea of burying himself. He would take his chances in the water.

That stupid girl must've gotten scared and ratted on him, he thought as he continued his run towards freedom. It was a gamble to ask for her help in the first place, but he was out of options. He needed help and thought she could be trusted. Just one more person to add to the list of people who had betrayed him throughout his life. If he hadn't insisted on checking her car after she brought the supplies in, at least he'd still be able to fortify himself inside the cabin. Now there was nowhere to go except the river. Damn! He muttered again. How many more mistakes can I afford to make before I end up dead?

The forest was beginning to look more and more familiar the deeper he got into the thick of it. He knew the river's edge was no more than 100 yards in front of him, but he wasn't prepared for the frigid waters. He didn't even have his jacket on him. Not that that would help once in the water. Less is more, especially in white water rapids. All a jacket would do was weigh him down and make his swimming motions that much harder to control in the fast moving current.

Closing in on the banks of the river, he thought he had his mind made up. Realizing the temperatures of the river would do more harm than a bullet from one of the guns that was after him, he reconsidered. He needed to think in a hurry. He needed more time. But time was something he didn't have the luxury to rely on right now. He was out of options.

He could hear the shouting from the search party nearing. He needed to make a decision now. Go for broke and try to swim for the other side, or head back into the woods to wait the search party out. Not much of an option either way you look at it, he thought.

Taking one more glance at the icy waters in front of him, he retreated to the one place he felt he could hide and wait out the incoming threat from the police officers. He just hoped he wouldn't freeze to death first.

GreaT FaLLS, VA
December 22nd, 4:01 PM

W ithout a second thought, I was off the porch and after him. Heading into the darkness of the forest in what I hoped was the same direction that he had fled to. I ran at a speed I haven't hit in many years. Dodging low-hanging branches, fallen trees and rocks slick with wet moss, I was at a direct disadvantage with the loafers I was wearing. Not to mention I had no reference as to where I was headed. This deep, thick forest was about as foreign to me as if I were plucked up and set down on the surface of Mars.

I was a bit scattered, too. My adrenaline was still at record highs after the near miss from the bullet back at the cabin. Hoots from the owls and calls from the night birds echoing through the trees had me on edge as I ran blindly through the woods. The sound from the rushing waters of the falls was my only guide, though it hardly gave me the direction that I needed to take. I took a glance backwards to find not only Diamond right on my tail, but Jack, McFweed, and a dozen or so other uniformed coppers there, too. Thank God. I'd hate to be lost in this maze by myself.

I kept after the sound of the water, thinking that it had to be his only path to escape. At least I hoped it's what he was thinking too. There would be no way to find him if he stuck to the forest. Not at nighttime, at least. Our only hope of catching him was going to be if he was out in the open where we could see him. Then there's the Potomac that we will have to deal with too, though he'd be a fool to try to make a break for it by swimming across the river. If the icy cold water didn't kill him, then the rapids of the river surely would pulverize him like a tomato in a blender. I didn't see a route to freedom for him. Either he stayed under the cover of the trees and risked the near-freezing overnight temps, or he opted for the water. Either way, it looked to me like his only chance for survival was giving himself up.

I was running through the forest blindly with no trail to speak of in front of me, not even knowing which direction I was headed in. We were burdened with not knowing a thing about these woods, while Embry ran through them like it was a walk in the park. I sensed I was losing ground on my prey, but I kept trudging on. Regardless of how many scrapes my face was taking by the low hanging tree branches I kept running directly into.

A minute later, I finally caught a break. I came to the platform that was set up for people to admire the beauty of the waterfall. It's like it was the middle of the afternoon all of a sudden as they outfitted the structure with flood lights bright enough to make the Vegas Strip jealous. I could finally see my surroundings as clear as day. Hard to believe we couldn't see this much light through the trees.

The observatory jutted out over the waters below by a good fifty to sixty yards. But there was still no sight of the man that I was chasing in any direction I looked. Stumped and deeply out of breath from my run through the forest, I took a pause to catch my breath. With my hands on my knees as I hunched over, the rest of the group tailing me finally caught up.

"Anything?" McFweed asked.

"I got nothin, Ted," I respond with labored breath. "I don't even know if he came this way. But as you can see, it's just us out here now."

"Let's split up," he suggested. "You and Diamond go out to the end of the platform and scan the area. Me and a Jack will go as far down the side of this thing as we can. I'll direct the rest of the crew to keep an eye from the cusp of the trees. If he's out here, he ain't gettin' by us."

The sound from the waterfall was so loud that I couldn't think. *Where would I go from here?* I asked myself as I watched the rest of the men fall into place after McFweed's orders were barked.

There was nowhere else he could've gone, unless he hooked a u-turn back in the woods and outmaneuvered me or took a dive off of the platform. Slowly, I inched myself closer to the ledge of the platform. Diamond was right behind me for the first time since we were shot at. His breath laboring as hard as mine. I pointed to the opposite end of the terrace, wanting him to have a look over the edge on that side. I stayed where I was, surveying the vista for any movement.

I reached the edge of the platform, looking directly below me at the rushing waters underneath. I looked both up the river and down, towards the shores on my side and the other. No sign of him anywhere. Dumbfounded, I started back toward where I first met the rest of the group of men rushing towards me a few moments earlier. McFweed pointed down below and I quickly grasped what he was pointing towards.

While Cole and I walked to the edge of the platform, McFweed and Jack tried to make their way down the side of the embankment. Underneath the observation platform was a makeshift scaffolding setup.

I made my way down the side of the structure, thankful for the metal bars that were rigged up around me. They must have been out here doing maintenance on the platform since it was the off-season. Regardless of the reasoning for it being there, I was glad it was.

I noticed a slight movement as I followed McFweed. Something that caught my eye as I traversed down the slick rocks. The floodlights were an absolute godsend as I noticed it was Embry that I saw. He looked to be hanging on for dear life to one of the metal bars, slick and damp with moisture from the mist of the waterfall below.

Jack was already halfway out onto one of the wooden planks that had been set up for the workers. I was amazed at his bravery. This is the same man that wouldn't walk a block to go question a witness, and yet here he was, playing the hero on an ice-covered scaffold setup.

"Jack!" I screamed. "Be careful out there. It doesn't look too safe."

"He's right here," he shouted back, "I'm almost to him."

Not wanting to risk an accidental fall from my friend, I pulled myself up onto the plank and inched my way towards the two of them.

"Horace Embry," I shouted at the man, trying my hardest to make my voice cut through the noise of the rushing waters below. "Stay where you are. We will rescue you."

"Stay back!" He warned. "One more step and I'll let go."

"You don't want to do that, Horace. We can save you," Diamond yelled from directly behind me. I was so focused on Jack and Embry that I didn't even notice he followed me out there.

"I don't want to be saved. I don't deserve to be saved. You saw what I did to those girls. God will not forgive me for those sins."

Though he was still too far away to make out his facial expressions, I could hear the trembling of his voice. He was frightened. Without doubt, either. One choice was to let go and end it all. The other was to hang tight and be brought into justice. Not really a good option for him either way.

I continued inching closer on the scaffolding. All the time, keeping my eyes on him to make sure he didn't jump.

"Horace, I can reach you. Just hang on for another minute," I shouted, hoping that he would listen to the reason in my voice.

I passed Jack on the plank and continued moving forward, one small step at a time. The ice buildup out there was incredible. I was slipping with nearly every step I took, even though my hand hadn't left the pole surrounding the makeshift walkway the entire time. Diamond knelt down and began to crawl the rest of the way. I let him go by me. He seemed to navigate the slick platform better than Jack and I were. He was only about three feet away from Embry now. I was still a full two steps behind that.

A rock formation that jutted upwards towards the base of the platform meant the riggers had to get creative when erecting their scaffolding. It created a bit of a fork in the road, if you will. Diamond continued crawling on the path that he was on, while I took the longer route around the giant rock that interrupted my path. With Embry focused on the crawling Diamond, this gave me the chance to sneak up around the other side of him without notice.

"Hold on Horace," I said to him as I knelt down beside him. "I'm right here. Give me your hand and I'll bring you back up."

I reached out with my left hand, securing my grip on the metal pole in front of me. I used the leverage to put one foot onto the wooden board that he was closest to. My feet were slipping on the damp wood.

If there was no traction on that, I couldn't imagine how slick the pipe was that Embry was clinging to.

"Stay back!" He screamed again. "I'm warning you, one more step and I let go."

Thinking he was balking, I pushed off with my free foot and got my whole body onto the platform that he was hanging from. I reached out with the entire length of my body to grasp his hand. Jack and Diamond both right behind me now, holding onto my legs for extra support.

I felt my fingertips touch his just as he lost his grip and fell below. The look on his face is one I don't think I'll ever be able to forget. Sheer terror shone through his eyes as he dropped. I looked over the edge, past my outstretched hand as his body fell faster than anything I had ever seen before. Gone. Into the whitecaps of the rushing waters below. I caught one last glimpse of his head bob up above the waterline before it whisked away his body down river.

"Go, go, go!" I turned and shouted at McFweed. Though I knew it was over.

Diamond and Jack took off back towards land as I sat cross-legged on the damp wood with my head between my hands. I was so close. If only I was a split second earlier, I could've saved him.

After a few moments, I finally got up and aided in the search efforts. I made my way down to the shore of the river, hoping for another sight of the man's head in the water. But I knew it was no use. We wouldn't be bringing him in. Our only hope now was for a recovery of the body. Nobody could survive that drop.

Great Falls, VA

December 23rd, 12:45 AM

The Virginia State Troopers called in the local search and rescue outfit to aid us in searching for Embry. We were out there nearly the entire night before McFweed called us off the chase and directed us to return home. It's not easy trying to find someone under the cover of darkness in roaring white-water rapids.

Officer Barros followed Ms. Watson home after we informed her that Embry had fallen. I told her I didn't think he made it, which she met with a half-smile as she welcomed the thanks that I had given her. If not for her, who knew how this would've ended for us?

Search and rescue continued their efforts, with men on either side of the river for a two-mile stretch throughout most of the night. The only thing that was recovered by the time Diamond and I left the campground was Embry's left shoe. That told me everything I needed to know—backing up my theory that didn't make it.

Jack said he was going to stay on and help with the recovery efforts when Cole and I finally left the campground at a quarter after one in the morning. I wasn't optimistic that he would be successful, but if he was drawing a paycheck from the MPD—however slight it may be—I gave him credit for sticking it through.

Once daylight broke, the search and rescue efforts became focused on recovery instead of rescue. They dragged the river that whole day without even a trace of Embry's body. That seemed suspicious to me. I thought surely they would recover something by the end of next day, but no body was found.

There was no way he could've survived that fall. Not when there were boulders the size of fire trucks directly under the observation platform. My guess was he got caught up in a mess of debris that the beavers had brought down to make their dams with. If that was the case, the only way he would be recovered would be if they drained the entire river. And we know that's not a possibility.

I took that knowledge to the families of the four girls and apologized for not being able to bring their murderer to justice. The consolation was that I offered them the solace that he could never hurt anyone ever again at the same time. The tears in their eyes were indifferent. And I don't blame a single one of them for it.

Sure, they probably felt blessed that Embry met his maker, but there's no finality of justice quite like seeing your child's murderer being led away in handcuffs to a lifetime behind bars.

Without a body, it will probably be in the back of all our minds for a while that maybe he made it. That there's a possibility—however slim it might be—that he made it out of the river to dry land undetected. Eluding the hundreds of men that were searching for him that night and the dozens of law enforcement officers that held a perimeter around the campground. But I guess we'll never know.

The rest of the week was a pretty somber time for all of us. Jack checked in with me on the daily, saying that he wasn't going to give up the efforts until they found Embry. Dead or alive. I commended his ethics. I, unfortunately, wasn't given that same benefit.

Diamond and I were handed another case two days after we returned home from Great Falls. An open and shut case that we solved in record time.

A man was robbed at gunpoint in Georgetown, taken for everything he had on him—including his clothes.

He vowed revenge and got it that same night. Running down the man who robbed him with his work truck. There was brain matter and body parts strewn all across P Street.

A witness had written down the license plate number of the work truck, giving us an address for the man. We arrived at his house around eleven that night and hooked him up after he admitted to everything.

Cases weren't always as cut and dry as that one was, but it sure helped our psyches after the ordeal of letting Embry slip through our hands earlier in the week.

One week later

The girls' bodies were all returned to their hometowns for services and burials by the end of the following week. Not forgotten here, their friends held a vigil for the four fallen students in the university's courtyard on the day before the last day of the year. A fitting send off for what will be a year that all of these people will want to forget.

Diamond picked me up at ten minutes to nine on the morning of the service. Sarah booked it out of the house in the nick of time, probably passing Cole out on the street as she drove away. Which gave me a quick second to find my last bottle of scotch that I had stashed in the floorboard by the front window. If I was going to go to a wake, I needed some sort of liquid courage. There's nothing worse than seeing the sadness of people grouping together to mourn a loved one. Especially when you're an outsider who sticks out like a sore thumb.

The Howard University choir was on hand and performed a very moving rendition of Amazing Grace that left every single person in attendance with damp eyes. Myself included.

Only one of the girls' family members was present at the service; the mother and younger brother of Ruby-Sue Daniels. I made small talk with them as we waited for the ceremony to begin, contemplating whether or not I should clue them in on the toxicology reports that Allcott had given me a few days earlier. Ultimately, I kept it to myself. These people had been through enough already as it was. I didn't want to burden them with the fact that their daughters had been poisoned before they were murdered. To me, that seemed like adding insult to injury.

Each of the four girls had traces of fluothane in their systems, which was most likely why they didn't fight back. After an inspection of the three remaining wine bottles that were collected from the house, Frank determined that there was enough of the poison injected into each bottle to subdue a rhinoceros. Which was another reason for me to keep that knowledge to myself. The act of murder is a cruel enough action that I didn't think the families needed to hear anymore.

As the ceremony was winding down, I spotted Jimmy Malone and Boyd Perkins in the crowd and approached them.

"Jimmy," I said with as much of a smile as I could muster for a situation as depressing as this, "I'm glad everything got sorted out."

"Me too. I want to say thank you for believing in me. Not many police officers would have, especially given the circumstances."

"The job of a detective is to follow the clues that are given to us," I explained. "In this case, unfortunately, they led to the both of you, but they also told me you weren't the man we were looking for. I never stop until I'm satisfied that I have the right man. Never."

"I appreciate that. If you didn't listen to me, I'd still be rotting away in that jail cell right now."

"Well, I listened to you, Jimmy. And besides what you told me about Ruby-Sue and this case, you also told me you were eager to find a better life. Is that still correct?"

"Yes. It is," he explained. "I found myself while I was behind bars. That's not how I want my life to turn out. So, I'm gonna do right by Ruby-Sue. And myself. I've seen the inside of a jail cell, and I never want to see that again. I've even enrolled in the university here. I know I've got a long way to go, but it's a start."

"That's great to hear, kid. I hope everything works out for you. Here," I said while fishing a card out of my pocket, "take this. It's the phone number of a good buddy of mine. I can't say that he'll take you on but give him a call. He's a P.I. Even if it doesn't work out, it doesn't hurt to chat with him."

"Thanks Mr. Denver. I sure will."

Jack approached the three of us while we spoke. I didn't want to put him on the spot, so I waited until Jimmy and Boyd took their leave before bringing up the fact that I gave the kids his business card.

"I think you should think about it, Jackie Boy," I said after explaining the situation. "Those kids need a fresh start. Jimmy knows he's made some poor decisions in his life and wants to atone for them. Just sleep on it for a few days."

"Ok, sure," he said reluctantly. "But I ain't making you no promises, Maxey. I had to deal with you for most of my career. What makes you think I want to train another nitwit who will end up being a royal pain in my tush?" He said with a laugh.

"Just think about it," I returned. "That's all I ask."

Conversation turned to something else as I spotted Sarah off in the distance. I thanked Jack for at least giving the idea some thought and headed over towards her in the parking lot.

"Well hello there, doll face. What's a pretty girl like you doing hanging around a place like this?" I said with a grin.

"Oh, you know. Just seeing if there's any single coppers who might wanna take a ride with me is all," she returned with that look that drives me crazy. "So, what do you say, Flattie? You wanna take a ride with me?"

"Absolutely," I said as I opened her car door for her.

I smiled to myself as I walked around to the passenger side of the car. This case wasn't a fun one, not that many of them are. But it taught me a valuable lesson about making sure that your loved ones know you love them. You never know when it might be the last time that you see them.

It's hard to check your bags at the door when it's time to go home. But this little lady was helping me learn the difference between a work life and a social life. I haven't perfected it yet, but we had the whole rest of the day to practice. If I'm going to get back to the domesticated lifestyle, I'm going to need as many lessons as I can get.

I took one last look at the crowd that was gathered in the university courtyard. Jack was still in the same spot I left him at, watching me as I got in the car with Sarah. I guess the cat's out of the bag on that one. I'm a bit too old to be hiding the fact that I have a girlfriend, anyway. Besides, if that was the worst thing to come out of today's service, then I'm a lucky man. Unlike the families of those four girls, I still have all of my loved ones accounted for. As true of a blessing as there ever was.

EPILOGUE

The doors of the service station flung open with enough force to shake the windows, as the bell that was hanging from it torpedoed its way to the floor below. Stepping over it, he continued inside, past the shelf that held various brands of oil and other car supplies, as he made his way towards the front counter. He wasn't interested in any of that while he squinted to see the person behind the counter from the early morning sun that was shining through the door behind him.

He was lucky enough to be able to even walk through that front door. After letting go of the icy pole he was hanging onto, it was a miracle that he was able to still stand on his own two feet. A drop like that would kill most men. Instinct took over as his paratrooper training returned mid fall. His body became as straight and as narrow as a flagpole, making the inevitable impact with the water as seamless as possible.

His only struggle, besides eluding the search party, was when he became ensnared in some tree branches that were collected against one of the massive rocks below the scaffolding. Which ended up ultimately helping his escape efforts as the rescue team focused their efforts down river, thinking he was swept away with the currents. It was a quick swim back to the base of the observation deck after he saw that the shore was left unmanned by the authorities. Once back on dry land, he continued his escape upstream in the opposite direction of the search team.

This was the first person he had come across in quite some time after he pulled himself out of the rapids of the river and stumbled through the forest back to civilization. He felt this was a chance brought down from the heavens above, and he was going to make sure to take full advantage of it.

His head had stopped bleeding the day before, but the pain was still enough to drive him mad. His left eye was swollen and crusted shut by the pus and dried blood that had accumulated over it, making it hard for him to see too clearly. He was having a hard time figuring out if the sights in front of him were real or if they were figments of his concussed mind. Playing more tricks on him like they had been when he was searching for refuge in the forest, and he came across the carcass of a dead deer instead.

This all seemed too good to be true, but he knew it had to be now or never. He had lost one of his shoes in the fall, and the sole of that foot was welted and raw from traversing over the rough terrain with no cover. There wasn't much more he could do before the infection became too far gone to heal. He needed to do something now to ensure his survival.

After peeking in the window of the lone car in the parking lot before going into the store, he knew what his plan had to be. Take the person inside for all they had and make another run for it. After the fall that he took, he knew the cops must've thought the worst and called off their search. A dead man doesn't need chasing, after all. This right now was his best chance to finish his escape. It was just too risky to head back to the campground to retrieve the loot he had stashed there.

The woman behind the counter cowered as he entered. She knew bad news when she saw it, as his appearance sent shockwaves throughout her body, prompting her to reach for her piece beneath the counter. This wasn't the only vagrant that had wandered into her store. Being the only place to fuel up on a lonely highway almost guaranteed some sort of riff raff would come through from time to time. But she had never seen a person as rough as this guy seemed to be.

"Don't," Embry said as he saw her reach under the counter. His voice was as sharp and lethal as the bullets inside of her gun. "Just give me what I want and I will be out of your store."

She kept her eyes on him as she slowly pulled the gun up and into view. "And what exactly makes you think I'd do a thing like that?" She said confidently. "Look at you. You look like you were hit by a train. If I blow on you hard enough, you'll fall over. What makes you think I should do a damn thing that you say?"

He said nothing in return as he continued to step closer and closer to the counter that separated the two of them.

"Stay back or I *will* shoot you," the woman said as she refused to back down. She raised the gun up to chest level as she spoke, letting her guest know that she wasn't balking.

With her arms held straight out in front of her, she closed one eye as the other looked down the barrel and took aim at her intruder. Wordlessly, she walked from her side of the counter out into the open space of the store. This wasn't the first time she'd had to pull out her weapon while on duty, but then again, she'd never been face to face with someone as ruthless and desperate as Horace Embry was, either. Hopefully, her brazen efforts wouldn't backfire, she thought as she refused to take her eyes off of the man.

Embry took four steps forward, unafraid of the weapon whose sights he was now the focus of. As the jaw of his assailant tightened, he made his move.

"Just give me what I want and I'll be on my way. I don't want to hurt you, but I will most definitely defend myself until the end," he warned her once again.

She stood tall and held her ground. She knew she still had the cigarette machine to duck behind if she needed to, but she held the upper hand. She had the gun. She had the power. Or so she thought.

In one quick thrust, he had covered the remaining three feet of space that separated the two of them. Disarming the woman as she fired a round into the ceiling and taking her in a choke hold simultaneously. He knocked her hand against the cigarette machine, which made her lose control of the weapon. He winced in pain as he used the big toe of his bare foot to corral the weapon that had landed a few feet away. Using the weight of the woman to his advantage, he leaned down to pick up the firearm while he kept her pinned up against the cabinet.

"You should have listened to my warning," he screamed as he took her gun in his right hand and jammed it against her temple. "Now you're going to wish that you did."

A slight and muffled scream escaped her lips as she pleaded for her life. "Take it. Take everything. Just leave me alone."

He mulled over the request for a split second before he pulled the trigger without another thought. A clean kill. One bullet to the temple. Just like he learned in the Army.

Discarding her limp, lifeless body onto the floor at his feet, he stepped over her, continuing on with his plan. He rounded the corner of the counter and took the contents of the till and the first aid kit that was in the cupboard below the register. He could feel the warm fresh blood from his victim's wound dripping from his face as he bent over her dead body and retrieved her car keys.

He got to work fast, scrubbing his face first, then cleaning the sole of his foot before taping it up with gauze. Driving would be tricky with the taped up foot, but he didn't have any other options. He needed to flee the scene before another car stopped by. Though he felt bad about taking her life, he really was left with no choice. He couldn't leave her alive, not after she had seen his face. Not if he wanted to remain free. It was him or her. Which was an easy decision for him to make when it came down to it. Survival of the fittest, is what he thought.

With a clean face and a fresh shirt that he grabbed from the back seat of the car, he stuck the key into the ignition. The engine turned over on the first try and he made his way back to the road.

He didn't know what town he was in, or even which direction he should go. But he drove on anyway. Not that any of that mattered. He had what he had come for. The perfect vehicle for his escape.

ABOUT THE AUTHOR

Tyler Craig hails from the great state of Washington, though he now resides in the desert southwest in the Phoenix metropolitan area. He developed his love for writing about 15 years ago having started out in journalism, before trying his hand in fiction. With more than two dozen short stories, novellas, picture books and full-length novels under his belt, Mr. Craig strives to become your next favorite author. For more information on Tyler Craig, including news and upcoming projects, stop by tylercraigauthor.com

If you enjoyed Slash and Grab and would like to take a few moments to leave a rate and review, you would make this author very happy. Independent authors don't have it as easy as many of our traditionally published peers, so each rate and review go a long way towards getting our names and products out into the world a bit easier. Thank you.

ACKNOWLEDGEMENTS

As always, I want to give a huge thanks to my family for always believing in me and pushing me to never stop creating. If not for their love and support, you would not be reading this right now.

I also would like to give another huge thank you to my editor, Kassi Mackey. I literally went out on a limb and asked if she would be willing to work with me on this project, and I honestly think I have found my editor for life.

Thank you to my resident law enforcement liaison, Marcus Callahan, who's patience in my never-ending text threads during the writing process deserve a gold medal.

And last but not least, I would like to thank Leslie Mainer, Pete Martin and Lucy Johnson, who root for my success probably more than I do.

ALSO BY

DC Homicide

Inspector Harley: The World's Greatest Pet Detective